HYPER OBJECT

Volume 1

Written By

Shae Moloney

Created By

Kyle Keller & Mark Sidener

outer
giant

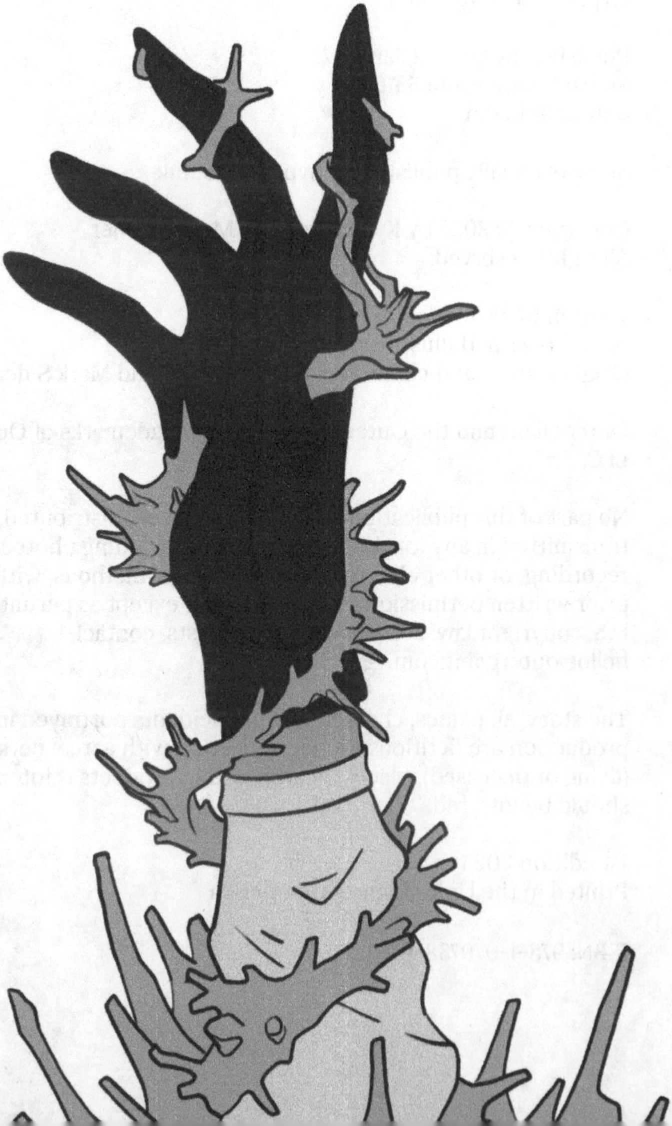

Hyper Object Volume 1

Published by Outer Giant LLC
St. Paul, Minnesota 55104
outergiant.com

Story originally published at hyperobject.ink

Written by Shae Moloney
Book Cover and Illustrations by Matt Owen
Original story and characters by Kyle Keller and Mark Sidener

1st edition 2025
Printed in the United States of America

ISBN: 978-1-970738-00-1

Contents

CHAPTER 1

Lees the Mite

I

Lees had been twenty for less than three hours when she was abruptly woken by a knock at her door. The silence that followed had palpable weight, like the calm before a storm. Her half-asleep brain teetered on the edge of indecision – get up or fall back asleep? But then the sound of closed fists pounding furiously broke through the fog and forced her to stumble out of bed.

The pounding continued as she shuffled forward. When she finally made her way to the entryway, two readily armed chippers crowded the doorway. Their mouths moved, but Lees couldn't quite make out what they were saying. Then their hands extended toward her, and they offered to escort her to the train station, more of a statement than a request. Two steps backward, and she could have darted out the back door, but she found her legs moving forward without her consent. She watched her feet, now clad in boots she did not remember putting on, shift from aqua tile to the gray carpet of the hall and then the crimson pavers outside. The chippers' rugged hands clasped tightly onto her shoulders as they led her down the neatly paved pathway, away from the only home she had ever known.

Lees studied the strangers whose fingers were driving bruises into her skin. The older man was just doing his job, she decided. His round face was sullen and weathered with reddish cheeks that indicated a love of spiced moss liquor. There was no joy in his expression, just resolve. The younger one, though, he enjoyed hunting mites. He was a sickly looking man with a too-thin frame that swam in his uniform. His eyes glimmered in what she could only describe as glee, as if feeding on her panic.

She considered running, fighting back, anything, but the younger man locked eyes with her, and it was as if she were trapped. Her stomach hitched as she stared into the blackness of his pupils, which widened and widened as he laughed until she felt herself swallowed whole. Lees' heart hammered, and she started to cry out –

Lees jolted awake tangled in her sheets. Again. The chippers' faces swam before her eyes in excruciating detail before her vision adjusted to the thin light coming through the curtains.

She was sick of this ritual. Most mornings, Lees would lie there in her little room above Teeg's repair shop, her thoughts spiraling and worming their way through the events of that day. The memories crashed in painful waves until she arrived at the face of her mother.

Wilta, that was her name. Wilta was crying.

No. *Weeping,* Lees corrected herself. Weeping and wailing as she clawed at the arms of the men while shouting her name. A last desperate attempt to stop the inevitable.

"Lees, Lees, my sweet! I love you!" Her mother had shouted over and over, then finally declared at the top of her voice, "I will find you."

But she wouldn't, not really. She couldn't. That was part of the deal, the agreement that kept life in the Quarters stable, kept Hyper workers productive, and kept bloodlines progressing into the future without the taint of a mite. There was no place for her there now that she was an adult, even if her mother did find her someday.

Until that morning, Lees had only vague ideas of what happened to mites when they reached adulthood. Nobody liked to talk about it, and why would they? Families blighted by one were too ashamed to speak of it, and those with normal children attuned to Hyper had no reason to worry about it.

So when Lees found herself in the train car all alone

– save for the chipper escorts pointedly ignoring her – all she could do was try to keep her breathing even and submit to this new reality. They rode deeper into the cave systems until arriving at what must have been the lowest level of the entire kingdom.

Two years had passed since then, but the memories of that dreadful day continued to steal precious hours of sleep every night. Lees sighed, knowing she couldn't delay getting up any longer.

Grumbling, Lees swung her feet out of bed but kept them hovering above the ground. She stared down at the faded green wool socks, smiling at the image of her mother bent over knitting them late into the night. She'd finished the day before her 20th birthday and had proudly presented them to Lees right away, too excited to even wrap them. As she did every morning, Lees carefully pulled them off her feet, folded them, and tucked them in the bedside drawer.

Then, wincing in anticipation, she bounded out of bed with bare feet and skittered across the freezing stone floor to the radiator where her work socks had been drying out from the day prior. She dressed quickly, trying to preserve the fleeting warmth she had felt moments ago in her bed. Lees pulled on the thick overalls and a baggy stitched sweater. Tucking her silver hair under the collar, Lees fitted a buff over her neck. Finally, she thrust her feet into the too-large work boots. They'd been hand-me-downs from Teeg when she had come to stay with him. Every time she touched them, she could hear his gruff voice in her head: *"You'll grow intu-em."* She kept trying to explain to him that she was in fact fully grown, but his response had been to put her in a headlock and laugh loudly as she swatted at him, assuring her, *"No one's done growin', kid!"*

II

Lees hated how quickly the rushing air in the mine drifts chilled the sweat on her body. Somehow, she was always somewhere between overheating and shivering. She paused for just a moment, allowing her hand drill to rest against the stone wall as she leaned her small frame against it. An errant strand of silvery hair fell onto her forehead, and she impatiently jabbed it back under her helmet.

The time to take three full breaths was the longest she'd allow herself to stop moving. Anything longer could garner attention, and there wasn't much down here less dangerous than that.

A line of inch-thick circles arched behind her drill as she worked her way around a small but dense node of Hyper. She was careful to only drill through the rock surrounding the Hyper and not the Hyper itself. It was tedious work. Other miners would usually pass over nodes like this, assuming the small size was valueless. The company, however, would make more money off this lemon-yellow node as it would sell for a higher price. Darker color meant denser Hyper, which meant more money in her pocket. That's the only fact that mattered to Lees.

Most of these guys couldn't spot the difference anyway, Lees thought to herself with a smirk.

"You're too precise," A mocking voice said from behind Lees. She looked over her shoulder without easing the pressure on her drill. Yon, a miner in his mid-thirties whose grizzled face made him look twice that age, was eying her work.

"It slows you down," Yon continued as he crunched down on an oat bar.

Lees pulled the drill out of the wall and let the weight of it rest on her leg. While her drill might have been older than most of the other miners', the bit and housing beneath the scuffed paint were pristine. If its outer appearance wasn't enough of a theft deterrent, she placed sticky labels in a uniform grid around the entire body proclaiming 'PROPERTY OF LEES - DO NOT TOUCH!'

She slid her large ear protection off and turned to the man with a raised eyebrow before responding, "What?"

"You're still way too slow," Yon repeated, then took an enormous bite of the oat bar. Lees eyed it enviously. Her next meal was still hours away.

"I'm not slow. You just think that because you're careless," Lees responded. She nodded pointedly toward Yon's drill, which he'd tossed onto the sizable pile of Hyper dust he had extracted. Many of the larger pieces had crumbled under the force of the throw and weight of the machine.

She studied him and tried to ignore the remaining oat bar in his hand before continuing, "Its frailty is part of what makes it so valuable, actually. If you were just a little more careful, you could keep more of it intact. See, the thing about fully fledged Hyper is-"

"Yeah, yeah, I know the line," Yon said dismissively. His cheeks bulged with the last hunk of his snack. "Just 'cause you grew up craftsman don't mean you're smarter'n us. We know this i'nt true Hyper, just the dust," He swallowed with enormous effort, then brushed the crumbs from his shirt. He waved dismissively at Lees' pile, then his, "But they only pay us for what we pull out of this wall, kid. It's too fragile, takes too long to get through the bedrock. Time is money. You want to waste both, be my guest."

The miner bent down and yanked his drill off the pile, causing more of the Hyper to splinter and spill out across the ground near his feet. She winced at the sight of wasted dust floating away in the stale air of the corridor.

Lees watched Yon place his drill on top of the deposit he was removing. There was so much Hyper left inside the hole he made by drilling directly into the crystal, but it was all lost in his haphazard approach. An invisible pressure pushed against her chest as she watched the man aggressively shift his drill back and forth, working the bit to break off another chunk.

"That fancy education of yours don't mean nothing when you're crawling down in the dark," Yon sneered, before ripping the drill back to life. Lees scrambled to put her hearing protection back on. She'd learned quickly that this was just how people were in mine towns. Teeg aside, Last Light was no exception. The deeper you go, the harder the people are.

CRAAANG!

Even though the shift bell was so loud it vibrated her teeth, it always brought an immediate smile to Lees' face. She slid her last, perfectly chiseled Hyper node out of the wall and hefted it into her Granby car with great care. Hers was overflowing with nodes of all sizes glistening under the static lights.

Yon had dropped to his knees to hastily scoop dust into his car. Like his drill, his railcar was in bad condition. The iron frame was riddled with small holes that allowed Hyper to slip out as it moved. She paused for a moment and considered helping him sweep up the last bit, but then she caught him glaring at her.

Lees grinned before hopping onto the pegs she'd installed on her car and yanking the lever. She swayed as it snagged the drag line running between the rails. The car, which was papered in stickers matching her drill, rolled smoothly along the tracks on freshly greased wheels through the drift into the main shaft. She held her breath as the foreman dropped her Hyper haul into the skip, silently checking that each node remained intact as it tumbled out. Lees accepted the slip of paper with her day's weight and corresponding pay, and just managed to squeeze into the cage before it began its first ascent of the evening.

When the first wave of fresh air smacked her cheeks, Lees yanked her helmet and hat off so it could run through her damp silver hair. She spread her arms to let the rolling air cool the sweat-slick parts of her body through her mining attire. Exiting the mine instantly lifted her mood, not only because her shift was over, but also because she was meeting up with Teeg right away, per his request.

Today was a particularly special day, and Lees couldn't contain her excitement anymore.

III

Lees burst through the door of Teeg's Repair Shop. The smile on her face had grown with each step on the way there, and she was practically cackling as she skittered inside and clamped the heavy door closed behind her.

"Teeeeeeeg!" She shouted.

The main floor of the shop was strictly for business. Every inch of the place, from floor to ceiling, was cluttered with machine parts, fasteners, grease, and a large assortment of tchotchkes he'd collected over the years. A trio of figures with wobbly heads bobbed next to the register when Lees stomped by.

Beneath the comforting stench of grease and oil, Lees noticed the sharp smell of pink root and spices permeating from the floor above.

"Is he making curry!?"

Lees yanked off her boots and raced upstairs, cradling them under one arm. She smacked against the wall as she hit the landing at full speed, the promise of the savory stew too much of a distraction. Lees dropped her boots just inside her bedroom door, nearly missing their designated mat, and slid into the living room on her socks.

"Uh-oh, she's home!" A deep voice boomed from the cramped kitchen at the back of the apartment.

"What did you make me!?" Lees shouted.

"I ain't making you nothing!" Teeg growled back.

"Well then, what *are* you doing?" She probed. Lees moved to slide open the kitchen door, but it resisted her – a large booted foot pressed against the other side, just visible in the tiny gap between door and floor.

Undeterred, Lees raised herself on her toes and hung from the small porthole in the door, trying to catch a glimpse of what Teeg was working on. The large man's back blocked her view of whatever it was.

"Quit hanging on my hinges!" Teeg griped. "And for your information, I am working on... Dannel's broken compressor."

"In the kitchen?" Lees asked incredulously.

"Yes, in the kitchen!"

Lees pitched forward. Teeg had removed his foot, and the door swung forward sharply. She grabbed the counter and managed to stop herself from falling on her face.

"Nice of you to give me a hand. Deglaze those roots for me, then get out," Teeg said, keeping his back to her. He covered whatever he was working on with a baking towel before turning to rinse off his hands.

"I knew it," She hummed happily. Lees poured a few glugs of cooking liquor into the iron pan and reached for the wooden spoon as it sizzled with smoke, heat, and a fragrant spiciness. She scraped the transparent roots off the bottom of the pan and expertly flipped them before returning them to the heat and lowering the temperature. The static coil of the burner shifted in color from a bright red to a deep maroon.

The coil pulsing with energy was mesmerizing. She stared at it, almost imagining she could see the currents of Hyper flowing through it, lost in thought. Lees jumped slightly as Teeg gently put a hand on her back and pushed her out of the kitchen.

"Go sit, curry will be done in a minute."

Lees slouched into one of the mismatched chairs at the dining table and watched the kitchen door swing lazily back and forth until it finally came to rest again. Through the porthole, Lees could see Teeg adding more ingredients to the pan. Steam billowed out and curled upward toward the vent in the ceiling.

She sighed. Teeg seemed his usual self. With nothing else to do or look at, Lees' thoughts swarmed from all sides, hijacking her mood.

Had he really forgotten what day it was? Or did he remember, but not care?

Was it not a big deal to him?

Lees tried to push that aside, but an unpleasant pit was forming in her stomach.

Would it be annoying to ask? It's not like I'm really his family, maybe it doesn't matter that it's been two years to the day since he invited me to stay...

Then – without warning – *maybe he regrets it.*

That one was too much to bear. Lees wrenched her eyes upward and leaned her head on the back of the chair to stare at the ceiling. She began tracing the cracked plaster lines from one side of the room to the other, slowly following each trajectory as it intersected and split from the others. Her eyes lingered on one jagged shape that perfectly mirrored the scar that ran along Teeg's nose and left cheek.

The scar was a mystery. Teeg was much older than Lees, at least in his mid-forties, and wasn't one to talk about his past. For all she knew, it could have been an accident. But there was something about him that made her question whether there wasn't some deeper meaning behind it.

Lees let out another prolonged sigh. She really didn't

know that much about him even after living under the same roof all this time.

Today wasn't that special, she told herself. Nothing ever changed down here, so what's another normal day? *She wasn't special.*

"Hey Teeg..." Lee called out. She tried her best to project, but her voice still cracked a bit.

"In your head again?" Teeg responded. Lees shifted uncomfortably in her chair. *Why was he so good at reading her?*

"No," She said quickly. Too quickly.

"OK, well that's a lie," Teeg said with a scoff as he backed his way out of the kitchen door. "It ain't much, but I hope you like it!" He shouted, turning to reveal the curry in one hand and a giant blue frosted cake in the other.

Lees' face lit up. She felt like bursting into tears, but forced a cough instead. "I- uh."

"Don't tell me you forgot! We have to celebrate the day you came to stay with me," Teeg said jovially. Lees scrambled to move the half-finished projects out of the way to make room for the plates.

Teeg had outdone himself with the curry. Thick pieces of potatoes and mushrooms swam in the creamy curry sauce, and he'd arranged flower-shaped carrot slices on the surface on top of the sautéed pink roots.

She pulled her eyes away from the beautiful dish to look up at the large, bald man wearing a tan apron lined with floral stitching. His eyes crinkled as he smiled proudly, though his smile faltered a fraction when he noticed the tears welling in her eyes.

"It's my favorite day of the year, and not just because we get cake," He said, then looked down and made a sound somewhere between a cough and clearing his throat. Lees swallowed hard around the lump forming in her throat.

"Come on now, don't let it get cold. Dig in!" Teeg proclaimed, then clapped his hands and reached for the crackle shards. He winked at her before palming the small edible stonelike chunks and cracking them over the cake. They sputtered to life, popping and fizzing over the blue icing before melting into its surface. The white frosting piped in a line along the edges of the cake dripped down the sides – a decorative, personal touch that perfectly captured Teeg's style.

"It's perfect," Lees assured him while cutting herself an enormous slice.

The two nearly made it to the end of their meal without disruption, a rare, peaceful moment, before a whining suction sound followed by a dull metal clank pierced through the room.

"Looks like we got mail," Lees said. She pulled one last spoonful of curry into her mouth, then she hopped out of her seat and sped down the stairs towards the source of the sound. She stood on the bottom step, avoiding the cold stone floor of the shop, and dislodged the hefty metal cylinder. Rushing air hissed from the cylinder's resting place at the base of the brass tubes piped along the building from the outside. One tube sent and one received, each one marked with a corresponding arrow.

Lees popped the lid off the tube and retrieved the small postcard from within. She placed the canister back in the tray and ascended the steps slowly as she read its contents.

BURGERMAKER BROKEN...AGAIN - PLEASE HELP — JEZ.

"Jez," Lees whispered to herself as she closed the apartment door behind her.

"What'd we get?" Teeg called out from the dining room through a mouthful of curry. Lees stood in the hallway, eying her boots before glancing down at the kitchen door.

"Uh, nothing important, I can take it," Lees yelled back. She tucked the note in her back pocket and scrambled to put her boots on.

"Wait a sec," Teeg called out. "Come here before you leave."

"Fine, but it sounds like an emergency," Lees replied.

"Jez can wait a minute," Teeg said, already knowing the request's recipient. Lees only ever jumped at the jobs Jez sent. He gestured at a carefully wrapped bundle on the table that hadn't been there before. Lees felt her cheeks flush from the combination of Teeg catching her running to Jez and the realization that he'd given her a present.

"It's cold out there. Figured you should have this," Teeg said. The words sounded rehearsed, but his voice wavered.

Lees gently pulled back the cloth covering the square gift to reveal a dark red overcoat. It was crisply folded with the collar and breast pocket on top. The wrapping had done its job to protect the fabric from fading or bugs. Lees gently ran her hand down the front of the coat, admiring the stamped brass buttons. Nothing she owned felt like this – the fabric was thick but soft to the touch.

"Teeg, where did you get this? This is such a nice coat," Lees looked up at him in shock. "We can't afford something like this."

Teeg swallowed hard and squinted a bit. "It's – was – Ila's."

Lees' eyes went wide. Teeg never talked about his wife.

"Oh... no. No, Teeg, I can't take this," She stepped back and waved her hands.

Teeg grabbed the coat and unfolded it. "It ain't doing no good in that chest," He said gruffly, then motioned for Lees to turn so he could slip it over her shoulders. The coat was big on her, but not by much. He ran his hand down the sleeve and gave her a hearty pat.

"Looks good on you," He said. Then, his voice dipping lower, he added, "Ah, she would have loved you."

Lees didn't cough this time. Instead, she let the tears come, hot and heavy with the tsunami of emotions roiling inside her. She plunged her face into Teeg's chest and sobbed. Today marked two years of her losing her home, her family, her way of life. Two years since she'd arrived in Last Light.

Now, today also marked the first time in two years that Lees cried.

CHAPTER 2

Welcome to Last Light

Lees pulled her new coat tight around her body as she climbed down the metal staircase leading from Teeg's shop out onto the next tier of the town.

Last Light was situated deep within a tall, narrow cavern. Unlike the Quarters where she had grown up, which was flat and wide, the entirety of Last Light was clustered around the sizable mine containing large nodes of Hyper and Rapidite.

There was a common saying that "the deeper you go, more riches await," but this was the deepest underground establishment Lees was aware of. If that belief in buried wealth held any truth, Last Light must have been the exception. The town's popularity had soared as more and more Hyper was pulled from the mine, but none of that resulted in better accommodations or living conditions.

It wasn't like *fancy people* were coming down from on high to grace Last Light with their fortunes – at least, that's what Teeg would say on the rare occasion he overindulged in vinium. *No,* he'd say in that low, slurred way, *that so-called population boom was from those wealthy benefactors sending their workforce here to nab some Hyper. They shipped 'em here to live in the dirt and grime with the rest of us while they hauled away our resources.* He'd go on and on like this until Lees gently helped him into bed to sleep it off.

What that influx of workers meant for Last Light was that people needed to build up instead of out. Maybe one day they'd scrape the rocky ceiling and have nowhere left to grow. Lees pondered this as she ran her gloved fingers against the cold stone railing on the edge of the third terrace. Each of the six terraces was inset from the one below it, making the whole town feel squeezed at the bottom. In theory, this allowed for larger walkways located on the front of each level, with homes and businesses tucked back further in. In practice, it meant that the more ostentatious builders could press the next building out further onto the edge. That annoying construction trend resulted in Lees needing to duck and dodge dense traffic, boxes, people, and shops every morning as she made her way down from Teeg's place.

There was talk at one point about building a tram system that would travel between the terraces so people could reach the center faster. Most of Last Light's inhabitants vetoed the idea, exclaiming nothing beats the ol' reliable carved stone stairs that their ancestors poured their sweat and tears into. The town begrudgingly settled on metal catwalks that stretched across the cavern to connect the two sides of the cave.

After two years, Lees had plotted what she believed to be the most efficient route from the fourth tier down to the ground: Right at Teeg's, down the catwalk stairs to tier three, left at the stone railing, through the food stalls, up over the stone railing, and down onto the staircase below. She'd timed it in her head. Hopping over the railing shaved off twenty seconds, which was great for speed but hell on her knees. From tier two, she'd race back to the center and find the next catwalk, clattering down like a frenzied mouse, rarely paying attention to anyone unlucky enough to be walking the same path. Finally, she'd reach the first tier where a descending zip-crate inched its way down to the ground level. She and Teeg had fixed the zipline enough times for free that the workers would just smile and look the other way whenever she hopped onto the moving crate.

Today, Lees reached the ground in record time. She paused to catch her breath, slightly regretting having basically sprinted the whole way. But the exertion felt good. The crisp air down at the lower levels chilled her lungs and made her feel stronger.

Her eyes drifted up towards the ceiling of the cave as she flexed her shoulders back. Supposedly, the Oppri's largest intact node of Rapidite was hanging from the top of this cave. The glowing stone bathed the entire town in a constant yellow light that Lees thought made everybody look a little sick. The Rapidite that hung in the Quarters was smaller but more clear, giving off a cool white light.

Lees' grandmother once told her that talented shapers had processed that stone in the Quarters. Intense, dedicated polishing revealed the true bright sheen underneath the dingy yellow.

Something to be learned from that, she'd said, pursing her lips knowingly at the spot just above Lees' head. The spot her grandmother always stared at when addressing her.

When Lees first arrived in Last Light, after she confirmed her eyesight wasn't failing, the stone felt like a source of some unknown infection. She'd glare up at the enormous Rapidite and wish for it to break loose and crash down on her, crushing her and the entire miserable town she'd be stuck in for the rest of her life.

On this night, however, she found the stone to be kind of beautiful. A soft, pale-yellow presence watching over Last Light and its residents. Maybe she was just feeling warm in her new coat. Lees skittered across the cluster of train track lines that bisected the town instead of walking down to the intended crossing. She wasn't the only one to take this route – someone had stacked bloom wood crates beside the elevated landing to act as steps despite the signs prohibiting the practice.

A warning bell rang out in rapid succession as the evening

funicular rolled into the station. Lees hopped up onto the landing and performed an exaggerated bow towards the frustrated operator.

She straightened up and locked eyes with a passenger close to her age. He stood directly in front of the door with a scowl on his face. Even through the cable car's dirty glass windows, Lees could see that his curly blond hair was freshly washed and styled. He wore an expensive-looking vest and gripped a ritzy duffel bag tightly with both hands. This boy looked like he was from the Oppri, or at the very least the Quarters, dressed in his holiday best.

He raised an eyebrow at her before turning his attention to someone else inside the car. His lip curled at the person's dust-caked jacket, and he angled his body away from them as much as he could in the crowded car. Lees' stomach turned. If this boy was a freshly-of-age mite arriving in town, she wanted nothing to do with him. She quickly hopped the railing of the station and dropped out of sight before the train doors opened.

Lees started forward but hesitated. The presence of an Oppri member was a rare sight in any mining town, let alone all the way down here. Jez was waiting for her, but Lees' curiosity got the best of her. She considered her options, but there was just no glamorous way to do this. Lees nestled herself between an overflowing trash bin and a discarded box on the backside of the station. She strained to hear through the clamor of passengers and workers spilling out on the platform, until two unusual voices cut through the chatter.

"She was looking right at me," A soft voice said. Their syllables were elongated slightly with an accent Lees hadn't heard in two years. "She must know something."

"I dunno, maybe she thought you were cute," A deeper voice responded, this one without a trace of the others' accent. "Let's get some food'n set a plan to meet with the mine chief."

"Alright," The softer voice agreed. "But keep an eye out for that girl anyway."

Woman, Lees corrected automatically. She pulled the rank-smelling bin further in front of her, mulling over the words. *Know something? What would an upper crestie want with me?*

The boy was much shorter than his companion and considerably younger. *Was this a bodyguard? Family member? Unlikely lover?* It was hard for Lees to discern the relationship from her vantage point in the garbage. The hulking man beside the boy walked with an unusually straight back and wore a dirty tan cloak that ended around his shins, exposing sturdy black boots that inspired no small amount of envy in Lees. His hair looked unkempt beneath a thick knit cap, the black and gray coloring matching his bushy mustache. The man's overall appearance was purposefully dingy and unassuming, but Lees could see the short blade tucked into his waistband and the embossed silver ring on his right hand that gave him away.

But what was a soldier of the crown doing in Last Light? Lees groaned. Whatever the upper crest boy and his cutlass escort were doing here, it couldn't mean anything good.

Lees watched the duo step down off the platform and inspect the bulletin board. Front and center was a large, flashy poster inviting all visitors to stop by The Eye of Mite, Last Light's best bar and only Hyper-automated restaurant.

"Well, wouldya look at that," The larger man said jovially, pulling at Jez's flyer. "A Hyper bar. Wasn't expecting that. Hard to believe they have a spinwheel working down here."

"The fact that they see this as their establishment's selling point and not the bare minimum is appalling," The boy sneered. His lip seemed to be permanently curled in disgust.

Wow, that kid sucks, Lees thought.

"This entire town is covered in garbage," He whined, using his free hand to hike up his pants to keep them from touching the ground.

"No it isn't," Lees muttered to herself.

"I wouldn't be surprised if the people living here lounge about in all this filth."

"No, we don't!" Lees grumbled before conceding that her current position among the trash did nothing to combat the accusation.

The duo headed into town and, to Lees' dismay, toward Jez's place. While she waited, she mentally mapped out the back alley path she could take to avoid them altogether. In just a moment, they'd round the corner and she'd be in the clear.

That is, until a miner spilled out from the bar on the opposite side of the road and crashed straight into the boy and his bodyguard.

"Eeeeh, we got a wee fancy boy here!" He jested as he swayed on the spot. "A little upp-errrrr crustie." His words slurred together, and he leaned forward to poke at the boy's vest.

"Don't touch me, you filthy grub," The boy growled. His bodyguard was already stepping between them before he finished the insult.

Lees winced, ready for the inevitable beatdown, but it never came. The cutlass man shifted the boy behind him smoothly and leaned his head down to speak with the drunk miner. Lees couldn't hear what he said, but the miner's face relaxed. He flapped his hands calmly toward the duo before turning to teeter away from the pair. Lees tensed again. There was no honor among the cutlass. A turned back was no different than a direct confrontation. Every cutlass she'd had the misfortune of meeting never hesitated to use force if the situation needed it – and every situation seemed to fit that bill.

But again, nothing happened. No right hooks, no knife in the gut, no hammer over the head. The two parties parted ways peacefully.

"That was weird," Lees mumbled. She half stood, half crawled from her hiding place with relative grace. An unidentifiable rotten peel stuck to her forearm, and she whipped her arm around harder than necessary to fling it off. It connected with the platform railing with a soft splat. An older woman sitting on a platform bench turned her head and gave Lees the stink eye.

The drunk miner reappeared from the other side of the funicular station, this time flanked by two other equally drunk men. Lees froze, and the woman behind her snorted.

"Hey, I had nothing to do with this," Lees snapped. The woman wrinkled her nose and made a show of turning away from her. "What?!"

One of the three men eyed her, but continued after the others down the street toward Jez's bar, presumably following the boy and his cutlass.

Lees bolted down the series of alleyways she knew would connect her to the bar in the most direct route. Roads in Last Light tended to meander and abruptly end, but the narrow alleys between buildings followed a grid system.

The back door to The Eye of Mite swung against the wall with a bang as Lees dashed through the kitchen and the swinging doors behind the bar. Midge glanced at her while arranging glassware behind the bar, grunting, "Mech's busted," before returning to the task.

"Yeah, yeah, I know. That's why I'm here," Lees said. She scanned the saloon. *Good, I beat them. I better warn* – Her face split into a wide smile and her train of thought vanished as her eyes landed on Jez.

The Eye of Mite's owner had been shockingly young when she bought the saloon. The folks at Last Light were skeptical when the establishment passed over to Jez, a newcomer barely 25 at the time, but within weeks, it became a hive of post-shift activity. The drinks were strong, the food was hearty, and the young proprietor was as charming as she was business-savvy. Drunks looking to brawl tended to frequent the spots closer to the train station and stay away from this spot, especially after the first night The Eye of Mite opened. Several broken fingers and a handful of concussions later, and Jez had proven herself as a force to be reckoned with when it came to handling rough customers. Teeg had told the story to Lees countless times, and she always smiled at his description of Jez wiping blood from her hands and announcing the next round was on the house if a few volunteers could help her carry some people out.

Jez hadn't noticed her yet, so Lees permitted herself a few moments to not-so-subtly admire the way she interacted with her patrons. Lees could scarcely remember a time when Jez actually stood behind the bar rather than sitting out with her customers. Today, a couple at the bar were laughing loudly at a joke she'd told after she triumphantly threw her cards down on the table. Jez tucked a few loose strands of long red hair back into her messy bun before collecting her winnings. Lees noted at least one gold ring in the pile.

Jez threw her head back to drain her glass. Lees' eyes widened as the woman chugged the full glass of amber liquid and felt her ears redden. The doors to the saloon opened, and Lees reluctantly pulled her eyes away from the beautiful woman. As expected, the strange pair entered the saloon with the three stooges from near the station following close behind.

Shit.

Lees reached for the closest thing at the bar – a shallow bowl of pickled tanglebug – and chucked one at Jez. It squelched loudly as it made contact with her arm. Unfazed, Jez wiped it away and locked eyes with her.

"Get. Over. Here!" Lees mouthed, motioning frantically toward her. Jez slowly, painfully slowly, stood from the table and sauntered over. She tried to maintain eye contact with the saloon owner and not let her gaze linger on the woman's rolling hips as she walked.

Stop it! Lees admonished herself. *This is serious!*

The moment Jez stepped behind the bar, Lees grabbed her and pulled her down. Jez kneeled next to her amongst the bottles on the bottom shelf and smiled at Lees, whose stomach flipped at the look.

"Lees?" Jez said, sending goosebumps down Lees' spine. "What are we doing here?"

"Uh...well, they and... um... sorry," Lees stuttered. She couldn't look at Jez's face, so she pretended to read labels on the bottles.

Jez placed a soft hand under Lees' chin and lifted it. She let her fingers linger there for a few seconds as she spoke.

"Is this about the mite and his cutlass henchman who just walked in here?" She asked.

"You... you know?"

"It's my job to know," Jez brushed some hair out of Lees' face. "Should we talk about this topside?" She grabbed Lees' hand to lift her up, but Lees jerked her back down.

"Did you see the drunks following them?" Lees asked, wide-eyed. "They were looking for a fight outside." Jez nodded.

"Yah, kinda hard to miss, especially this time of day," Jez said, nodding. She stood up again and pulled Lees to her feet with surprising strength. "It's nothing I can't handle. You go fix my burger bot while I take care of the situation."

Lees opened her mouth to recount the conversation she'd overheard, but stopped herself. It probably didn't matter. Whatever their intentions, Jez would snuff it out and send them packing one way or another. She shrugged awkwardly and headed toward the kitchen.

As the kitchen doors swung closed with Lees on the other side, Jez pulled a bottle from behind the bar and brandished it in her hand.

"Ah, there it is! Erish, you still want some peppermint? Go on – it's on me and the powers above."

Erish, a near-permanent fixture at the end of Jez's bar, hiccuped and accepted this gift bestowed from the heavens without question.

Focus up, Lees. Hungry people want food, and Jez is

counting on you, Lees thought fiercely, pushing her concerns into the back of her mind. She needed to dedicate her full attention to the broken machine. Working with Hyper-run machines required complete concentration, or things could go very wrong, very fast.

CHAPTER 3
The Eye of Mite

The Eye of Mite's kitchen was unlike any kitchen in Last Light. It had once been a standard, galley-style kitchen that churned out the usual bar fare, but when Jez bought the saloon, she'd retrofitted it to house something special: The Great Mechanized BurgerMaker 5000. This machine, referred to simply as "The Mech" by everyone employed there, was a squat, organ-shaped monstrosity that took up more than its fair share of space in the narrow room. Small, flexible pipes jutted out of it from all angles, each one winding its way around the kitchen to connect with custom rigs fitted over the top of previously manned appliances. Each of these rigs performed a task essential to making everything on the saloon's limited menu, all of which required just a tiny yellow Hyper crystal and a moderately talented spinwheel.

While Jez hardly let anybody just waltz into her kitchen, those who had seen Jeri work were typically impressed. His manipulation of the Mech's controls was akin to watching a musical performance, and most people were mesmerized watching him sling thick burgers, orders of crinkle-cut fries, and even a pretty decent milkshake.

Lees wasn't most people. She had a much different opinion of the entitled, lazy, good-for-nothing shaper who had no appreciation for what he worked with. Whenever she walked through the kitchen, she cringed at his stilted and jarring process that caused the Mech to rattle, shake, and grind against itself like an angry monster fighting for dominance over nothing.

Her feelings were not unjustified in her mind because his work often left the Mech in complete disrepair. Like today. The Hyper-operated Mech sat silently as she worked her way around the kitchen, carefully inspecting each station. The spatula arms jutted out at an unnatural angle, and the slicers, dicers, and even the spider-like claws that washed the dishes were stiff and retracted.

"Mech's busted," Jeri grunted. He didn't even lift his head from where he lounged in the hammock he'd strung up on the bar-side of the kitchen. Lees wrinkled her nose at his dirty boots that dangled over the produce washing station.

"That's what I heard," Lees replied. "What happened?"

"Dunno. That's your job," He said. Something rustled, and Lees saw he was paging through a newspaper. She looked around at the half-sliced burger buns lying on the counter between spilled curlicues of condiments that hadn't quite hit their target.

This asshole didn't even clean up after the Mech shut down, she thought with disgust. But it wasn't a surprise – Jeri had long ago made it clear he wasn't interested in lifting a finger to fix any of the problems he created.

Lees flattened her body against the counter to fit around the hammock so she could reach the machine's main board. She made sure to jostle the hammock and its occupant as much as possible.

"Please, don't get up, I wouldn't want to interrupt your important work," Lees grumbled.

"Can't do my job until you do yours," Jeri shot back with a flip of the page. Lees rolled her eyes.

"Could you pretend to care for once?" Lees muttered under her breath. She opened the main hatch and started inspecting the gears.

"What was that?" Jeri asked, shifting in his hammock to get a better look at Lees.

"Nothing," Lees' eyes slipped out of focus as she reached into the Mech, mentally visualizing its innards as her hand skipped along the gears, connecting wires, and other mechanical components. She leaned forward to reach her hand deeper and felt what seemed to be a large rod out of place.

Her fingers touched each rod as she counted, noting the space where the slipped one should have gone. "Ahh, did it shut down while you were working that fryer?

"Sounds about right," Jeri mused.

Lees sighed and guided the rod back into position. Once realigned, it smoothly slid into its housing and came to rest on a worn but functional gasket.

"Even though you use Hyper to control the different stations, there are still dependencies between them that work in tandem to your shaping," Lees lectured as she remounted the panel and began tracing the pipes over to the fryers.

"So you fixed it?" Jeri asked, sounding almost as if he genuinely cared.

"Not yet— you probably caused a bigger issue—" Lees trailed off to focus on detaching the arm mounted above the fryers. She looked down into the now-cooled oil and saw a mound of shaved roots that would never become crispy fries.

She slowly lowered the heavier-than-she-remembered arm onto a metal tabletop and then peered into the guts of the mounting box. Lees couldn't help but admire the craftsmanship. As much as she despised being around Jeri and his handiwork, she was happy to put up with him to spend time around this Mech. Every time she worked on a new section of the Mech, which was often, as Jeri was creative in how he mishandled and abused the machine, she came across something that blew her away. Lees didn't know what the Mech was *supposed* to look like straight out of the factory, because nobody down here could actually afford a company-manufactured one. Teeg has basically built the entire machine custom, and by now, Lees could recognize his style in the gears and tubing.

It was so intricate, with so much machinery compensating for the shaper in control. Lees wanted to toss this jab back at Jeri, but thought better of it. Who was she to insult a shaper?

"There it is!" Lees said triumphantly. She spotted a small sheared bolt that triggered a joining gear to fly loose and lodge itself against Jeri's Hyper, which was threaded through the machine. Without thinking, Lees reached out to touch the soft yellow strand before jerking her hand back, a small tremor of fear racing down her back as she did – *never lose your focus around Hyper*, she chided herself. She glanced over at Jeri, but he was lounging back with the newspaper draped over his face and both legs hanging lazily out of the hammock. She wasn't in danger of him activating it while her hand was in the way. He wasn't a concern at the moment.

The problem now located, Lees moved quickly. She pulled a small screwdriver from her belt and gently pried at the gear until it popped loose in her hand. Since Jeri was half asleep and not shaping it, the yellow thread of Hyper remained still. She set the gear back in place and grabbed the right-sized fastener to mount it once more, mumbling triumphantly, "*Now it's fixed.*"

An unmistakable surge of pride glowed in her chest. The

Mech wasn't always so easy to fix, and there weren't many opportunities for Lees to feel proud down in the mines, so she tried to savor the feeling as she hulked the large arm back into place.

She had just hopped down from the tabletop and was beginning to wipe her greasy hands on her pants when she heard the bar doors slam open. Seconds later, one of the enormous men from earlier came flying backwards into the kitchen, directly into Jeri and his stupid hammock. Their angry shouts bounced around the tiny room as the two rolled over one another, and the hammock flipped and dumped them to the ground.

Lees barely had time to finish laughing at the sight before the rest of them rushed through the door into the now cramped kitchen.

First came the snobby boy, who was also shouting while trying to avoid being trampled by the group behind him. His pristine shirt was wrinkled around the collar as if he'd been grabbed. Then came the boy's bodyguard, backing into the kitchen with both of his dinner-plate-sized hands around the neck of another man, one of the drunks that had followed the pair here. The man was clawing at his hands, but this was not a fight he was winning. The cutlass' face was eerily calm as he pressed his thumbs into the man's windpipe.

Finally, the last man from the group barreled through the doors, loudly slurring something unintelligible with his hands balled into fists. He was closely followed by Jez, Midge, and at least half a dozen other patrons who looked eager for a fight with the outsiders. Erish swayed toward the back, his reddened face half-hidden behind the bottle he was slugging from.

Guess this is Jez 'taking care of the situation', Lees thought as she pressed herself against the counter near the Mech to avoid the melee.

In seconds, the fight had spread to fill the kitchen. Eye of Mite patrons and outsiders seemed to be indiscriminately throwing punches and grabbing anything they could – forks, pots, rolling pins. One of the drunker patrons, who was clearly just looking for a good time, began shoving stale burger buns into his mouth while kicking anyone who got close.

Classic mine town fight, Lees griped. She pulled herself up onto the countertop at the back of the room just before Midge slammed a patron against the wall where she had just been standing.

Jeri staggered to his feet and pulled a crushed cigarette from his mouth. He spat tobacco onto the floor as he spoke, "That was my last Merric, you asshole!" He leapt onto the Mech's console, trying to get above the fight.

The hulking bodyguard threw one of the assailants across the room and into three other patrons, scattering them like bowling pins. It was impossible to hear anything over the cacophony of shouting and wet sounds of fists connecting with skin. Their shouts rose to a fever pitch as two more people charged the cutlass.

Lees scanned the room for Jez, who looked visibly fed up with the situation. The saloon owner leapt onto a table near the center of the kitchen, grabbed a pipe that ran parallel across the ceiling, and used it to swing around and land a staggering kick on a man who was wrestling Midge to the ground. Her foot connected with the side of his head, and he fell into a heap on the ground. Jez hopped down, sprinted toward the bodyguard whose attention was elsewhere, and clotheslined him.

"Hoo!" Lees gasped, her eyes going wide at seeing Jez move so quickly. She knew the woman could fight, had seen her in scrapes at the saloon before, but this was a whole new level.

Jeri let out a maniacal cackle, drawing Lees' attention. He had scrambled into position at the Mech and was looking at her with an unsettling grin.

"Let's fire it up!" Jeri shouted. He threw open the console, reached down, and yanked hard on the yellow Hyper. The strand stretched like gum and twisted in his hands. Lees was powerless to do anything except watch the saloon's cook-turned-fighter stand high on his marionette instrument and shout, "Eat shit, dirt bags!"

And the kitchen flared to life.

Plates, utensils, food, and condiments soared through the air and crashed every which way, throwing the fighting into a mob of chaos as people slammed into each other to avoid the assault. Lees couldn't tell which was louder, the shouts from the fight or the Mech screeching to life, desperately trying to perform its assigned tasks as its operator forced it to fight instead.

"Jeri! What are you doing!?" Jez shouted as a robotic arm swung right past her head and slammed into the drunk who had her in a chokehold.

"Saving your ass like always, boss!" He responded in a sing-song voice.

A sort of undignified yelp drew Lees' attention away from the Mech's crazed dance. One of the drunken fighters, now covered in salad dressing and burger toppings, was chasing the snobby boy around the kitchen trying to grab him. As frail as he appeared, the boy gracefully wormed his way through all the body-tackling and madness, throwing anything he could grab at his pursuer. Though it kept him a step ahead, the pursuer knocked away each item thrown at him with ease, forcing the boy to keep scurrying around the cramped room until he ended up right in front of Lees. He spun around, and grabbed a knife from the magnetic strip on the wall, and turned to face his assailant.

"You rich brat, think yer better'n us? Should've just given us what we asked," The man sneered. It was the same man the pair had encountered earlier. Lees watched the boy's face curiously. Whatever fear had been there before was gone. He looked more like a cornered animal ready to retaliate, and she wanted to be nowhere near these two when he did. The only problem was that they were blocking her exit.

Lees looked over and realized a control panel was still open. A small bit of yellow Hyper was exposed, the part that traveled up into the robotic arm she'd repaired earlier. She took a breath, concerned for her fingers, then quickly reached inside and yanked the single strand of Hyper. Like a muscle, the heavy robotic arm contracted and swung around, cracking the man in the back of the head. He toppled to the ground with a thud.

The boy whipped around and blinked at Lees, as if he hadn't seen her until that moment.

"Thanks," He said, sounding genuinely appreciative.

Lees ignored him to look around the kitchen again. The fighting was getting more desperate and violent as people dodged – or tried to dodge – the Mech's deadly parts between punches. Jeri seemed unfazed as he danced atop the console, positively beaming. If he had felt her tug on the Hyper, he either didn't care or hadn't realized it was her. The man twisted Hyper between his fingers like a puppet master, making the entire room move and dance to his whims. Lees had never seen him this happy while cooking.

The bodyguard reemerged, barreling past Jeri like a charging bull. He somehow had two people in a headlock, one under each arm. In a swift motion, he whipped both people forward and let go. The momentum carried the two towards Jez.

The saloon owner noticed just in time and gracefully leapt over the flailing bodies. They crashed into the wall behind her, knocking a few metal bowls off the shelf high above. With catlike grace, Jez climbed another counter and grabbed a skillet, spinning it in her hand before pointing it at the bodyguard.

"Alright, big guy, that's enough. You ready to cool down?" She said.

"Not happening. I'm simply ending this," The cutlass bodyguard replied flatly.

"Then I guess you're a problem," Jez said.

"Guess so."

Jez swung the skillet hard at his head. The man ducked, blocked the follow-up strike with one arm, then grabbed Jez's ankle with the other and yanked. Suddenly off balance, Jez's entire body dropped and smacked against the cold steel counter. Lees could hear the breath gasping out of her lungs. Without missing a beat, the bodyguard brought down his other arm right on top of her – but his forearm only made contact with the table's surface. Jez had rolled to the side, spinning over the arm that still held her ankle and kicking toward his face. Her foot landed with a thud as the bodyguard let go and staggered backwards.

Lees was already on the move. She raced across the room and, without considering the consequences, leapt onto the man's back. She was significantly smaller than him but still managed to yank him backwards by the neck. The two spun around the kitchen as the man tried to throw her off his back until he slammed her against a shelf full of produce that came tumbling down around them.

"My cabbages!" Jeri shouted. He sent one of the tracked arms speeding towards the bodyguard's gut. Lees let go and rolled to the side just in time to avoid the arm, but her opponent wasn't fast enough.

Jez gave a wave of thanks to Lees and stuck out her leg to trip a patron who was careening across the room swinging a sack of roots.

In the short time Lees had left the boy, he managed to get snagged by one of the drunks. The boy flailed and kicked wildly against the man who was trying to crush him with his grip. The man's teeth were bared triumphantly as he flexed his arms around the boy, too distracted to notice the dishwasher's gangly arms rising up behind him like a spider closing in on its prey. As the arms lashed out and latched onto his body, neck, and limbs, the man dropped the boy. The Mech pulled the struggling man into the sprayer box, which began shooting out pressurized water in all directions.

The boy raced across the room toward the barside door – the only exit not blocked by brawling patrons – but was intercepted by Midge. She spat blood as she wiped her face with a dish towel, then snapped, "Where do you think you're going?"

The boy gritted his teeth. "We didn't start this," He growled.

"Too bad. No one leaves till someone pays for all these

broken bottles," She stared him in the eye as she reached out to grab a bottle with her free hand and shattered it against the fridge, pointing the sharp end toward him.

Midge advanced on him. The boy scuttled backwards and into the corner next to his downed bodyguard, two of the drunken man's friends, and a handful of patrons Jez and Lees had finally subdued.

With that, as chaotically as it had begun, the kitchen brawl clattered to a messy halt. A single plate rattled to a stop on the tile floor, and then an eerie silence fell upon the room.

Those who were still conscious stared at each other, nobody quite sure what to do. That is, until a cacophony of chipper whistles and deep-voiced yelling erupted from both doors. A swath of local force poured in until every spare inch of the kitchen was occupied. Green-uniformed men and women grabbed people indiscriminately, pulling them apart and pressing them into separate corners while snapping commands.

Seconds later, the town chief hurried into the room, still hastily buttoning up his shirt and stuffing his tie into his back pocket.

"Break it up! This fight is over!" He shouted. The mass of motionless patrons and instigators stared at the man in confusion, but he didn't notice. He made a beeline for Jez, who tucked her hair behind her ear before placing a soft hand on his chest.

"Thank you for your help, Marshall," She cooed. The

man's cheeks reddened, and he pushed his chest forward slightly.

"Uh, well of course, Jez! Of course, happy to step in to keep you safe," He stammered.

"First round's on the house. We'll make sure every one of you gets a few drinks tonight for your hard work," She smiled softly, leaned in close, and finished buttoning his shirt. "And of course, your room is on me."

Lees' ears burned. She could practically see the steam pouring off the man's balding head.

"They didn't even do anything," She scoffed.

"What was that?" The chief barked, reluctantly turning away from Jez's won attention. Lees glared back at him. "You're supposed to be at the mine about now, aren't you?"

"No," Lees argued. "I already worked—"

"She was, sir!" The snobby boy suddenly piped up, affecting a lilting and stuttering tone. Lees stared at him as if he had transformed into a different person. "I'm - I'm new here and - and I was supposed to report to mine call."

"Are you ditching work, mite?" The chief glowered at her, squaring his shoulders and facing her fully now.

A deputy interrupted by calling over, "Chief, this big guy's hurt pretty bad."

Jez tried to step in, but the chief shushed her.

"Get to mine call now," He growled at Lees. "And take this kid with you."

Lees wasn't scared of the chief, even less so in a room full of people, but she knew the conversation was over.

The deputy shoved Lees and the boy out the back door, keeping a firm hand on their lower backs as if to keep them from running away. Lees stole one last look behind her. Jez winced and mouthed, 'sorry,' before turning back to thank the local force for their bravery. The chief began barking orders to arrest the drunks and get the bodyguard to the doctor.

Lees snapped her head back to glare at the boy, hoping to pour as much hatred and disgust into the look as possible. But where she expected to see fear, anger, maybe even anxious relief at not being arrested, she saw... hunger. The boy's eyes slid to the side to connect with hers, and he raised an eyebrow, his lips pulling back into a self-satisfied smile.

CHAPTER 4

An Unexpected Guide

When Lees and Meshi arrived at the ready room, the equipment manager didn't even bother looking up from their work to acknowledge them. They remained hunched over their tiny desk, jotting down notes on a clipboard. The wide ready room was more or less a glorified locker-lined cage bolted onto the cave wall. Half the lockers were open, each revealing a pneumatic drill – some pristine, others well-worn – dusty safety gear, and a chisel. Lees quickly crossed the room to a locker in the back corner and gathered her gear.

"You doing another shift, sparrow?" The woman asked Lees without looking up from her paperwork. Lees glanced at the woman, a hardened mine veteran who had worked her way up to the EM position in record time.

"Got sent down by the chippers, figured I'd make a show of it," Lees responded. She shoved a harness and a dented orange helmet into the boy's chest before beginning to strap herself in.

"Can't pay you overs."

Figures.

"Yeah, it's fine," Lees grumbled. She cinched the chisel harness around her thigh a little tighter than intended.

The boy stood unmoving in the center of the room, staring down at the dirty leather straps and rope in his hands with a look of disgust. His lip curled as he examined the sweat-stained lining of the helmet and studied the harness with mild bemusement.

"What's with soft hands?" The EM asked, jutting her chin in the boy's direction.

"Got his ass kicked. Chippers sent him down here with me."

"You got a name?" The EM called over. She had stopped filling out the paperwork and was rolling a pencil between her calloused fingers as she gave the boy an appraising look. A miner was only as good as the pile of Hyper he could mine, and this boy didn't look like much of a hard worker.

"Meshi," He responded, enunciating carefully and loudly. Lees snorted.

The EM studied him for a second longer before clicking her tongue in disapproval.

"Don't you die in my mine, *Meh-sheeee.*"

"How welcoming of you," Meshi muttered under his breath.

"This mite is your responsibility, little sparrow. Mistakes won't be comin' out of my paycheck," The EM extended her arm toward Lees and held out a tiny slip of paper.

"Yeah, yeah," Lees groaned. She snatched the slip of paper bearing their assignment, then tightened the band on the back of her helmet and gawked at Meshi, who still stood dumbfounded, holding the bundle she'd handed him.

"Quit standing around, soft hands, and grab some gear!" EM barked at Meshi. She slammed a hand down on her desk, and the sound rattled around the ready room. He jumped and scrambled to the nearest locker.

"Not that one!" Both women shouted in unison.

"Do you want Reggie to kill you?" Lees griped.

"Reg is probably the second worst person to snag gear from, right after little Miss Particular over here," The EM chuckled to herself before returning to her clipboard, the two mites forgotten.

"M'not particular. Don't mess with my stuff; I won't mess with you," Lees said. She slung her coveted drill over her shoulder, its neatly placed labels matching those on her helmet and harness, and watched the boy – *Meshi* – fumble to fit the harness and the other gear around his pristine outfit. Lees noticed with satisfaction he was already wrinkled and smudged.

The rusty cage squealed and shook as it descended into the mine. Meshi's face drew tighter and tighter with each passing floor. He had flat-out refused to get into the cage at first, calling it a metal death trap (a fair point, Lees had to concede), but the EM barked at him to *get the hell down into the mine before she threw him down the shaft*, and he had acquiesced, turning a delicate shade of green as he did.

"Shaft's deep," Lees said in a thick, folksy accent. "Quite a bit-a Hyper comes out a-here."

Meshi stared at Lees for a moment. "What is that? Are you doing an accent?"

"I was trying to be charming!" Lees said. Meshi turned away without a word.

"We actually *do* process a lot of Hyper from this mine. Even before coming here, I knew about Last Light. This is one of the most profitable mines in the whole kingdom," She continued proudly.

Meshi didn't respond. The lift operator raised an eyebrow, waiting for Lees to continue. She wondered if it was the word "profitable" that had intrigued the man.

"Well, when you pull Hyper from the tunnel's walls, you're actually... kind of chipping off a piece of a longer vein. For some reason, Hyper forms in wavy ribbons," Lees had now turned to face both men.

Meshi stole a glance at the other man in the elevator before responding. "I'm well aware."

"What's strange about ours, though, is the size of the veins."

"Why? Are they bigger?" The lift operator piped up. Lees smiled. At least someone was interested in what she was saying.

"You're getting it!" Lees shot a finger at the man with a smile. Meshi furrowed his brow. "They're so much bigger, like way, way bigger than any other Oppri mine. And no one knows why."

"Wow," The lift operator nodded thoughtfully. "You sure do know how to puzzle the old noodle, Lees."

"You sure know a lot about Hyper... for a mite," Meshi said softly.

Lees eyed him, certain the comment was an insult. There was a bite to the word when he said it, a tone she'd heard plenty before but never from another mite.

"Yeah, well, I learned it from my mom. Her father worked on some of the early processing machines."

"Your grandfather worked for OpLabs?" Meshi looked astonished. He finally turned to look her in the eyes, and Lees realized with a start it was the first time they'd made eye contact since she'd seen him on the train.

"What of it?" Lees asked. Her stomach twisted at the look he was giving her. She regretted saying anything.

Meshi's expression changed, his face softening as if in

apology. "No, no, I'm impressed. It's a rare honor to work there. You must be proud of that."

Lees could feel her face redden with frustration. Nobody ever complimented her mother's family. Even as a kid, her dad and grandmother dismissed her mother's work every opportunity they got. To finally hear a kind word about it, from this entitled boy, nonetheless? She gritted her teeth.

"What's it matter, anyway?" She snapped.

Meshi's eyes darted toward the floor of the cage. Then, perhaps realizing he could see straight through the metal grid to the yawning chasm below, his gaze settled on the railing. He reached out to twist a small bolt on the side of the railing. Was he embarrassed?

"I've always liked machines," He admitted. "But I was raised in the High Court."

"The High Court? No wonder you're so – wait, you're from one of the high-nine families!?" Lees blurted out. The lift operator's eyebrows practically disappeared into his hair-line as he whipped around to stare at the boy. Meshi lowered his head again and waved a hand as if to shut her up.

"Doesn't matter down here, does it? Privilege will only get you so far. I was... guided... to focus my studies on the art of Hyper, not machines. Forcefully. Because it was a more noble pursuit for someone of my standing," He practically spat out those final words.

Guided to study Hyper. Boo-hoo. I was guided to throw

my life away in the mines for the rest of my life, Lees thought bitterly.

Meshi looked crestfallen now, his eyes unfocused and lost in thought as he absently twisted the little bolt, and Lees's anger fizzled into something closer to shame and pity. Truth be told, they were both down here now. Whatever golden life he'd lived before didn't matter anymore. They were both victims of those in control deciding how they would live and what their lives would be like from now until their last days.

Lees considered patting him on the shoulder but couldn't bring herself to do it, so she cleared her throat before trying to comfort him.

"Sounds like your family... well, they suck," She finished lamely.

The cage screeched as it slammed into the ground, much sharper than was strictly necessary. Lees rocked backward on her heels to stop from tipping over. The operator chuckled to himself again. Meshi steadied himself on the railing before whipping around.

"Shut up! You don't know anything about them!" Meshi growled, eyes flaring. He balled his fists at his side, and Lees took half a step back out of surprise. "They're just traditional. Wanted what was best for me and the family."

He stomped off of the cage and into the main shaft. Lees stayed behind and watched him go, shoulders hunched and face twisted in anger.

"Seems you hit a nerve," The lift operator drawled. She

glared at him before stepping out of the cage. "See you in six hours!" Lees waved him off and followed Meshi into the mine.

The cage rattled and clanked back upwards, the sound following Lees as she headed deeper into the shaft. She hadn't been down here in at least six months, and as she rounded the corner, she remembered why that had been such a blessing. Each drift had its own foreman who had near complete control of how the work got done, so long as they delivered results. Eria's particular brand of control was notorious, and she'd never once gotten on his good side.

Is this our punishment for the kitchen brawl? Is the chief actually that cunning? What –

Lees' thoughts were interrupted by a loud, frantic noise echoing further down the drift. A flurry of voices followed. Her bulky equipment banged awkwardly against her legs as she ran forward and rounded the corner just in time to see Meshi being pinned against the wall by Eria. The foreman's sinewy arm pressed against Meshi's sternum was crisscrossed with X-patterned scars. She could never quite figure out what caused them and was far too smart to ask him directly.

"Get your filthy hands off me," Meshi hissed. He clutched a small satchel draped across his chest, the straps pulled taut by Eria's forearm. The foreman slid his arm up to press at the base of Meshi's throat. The boy made a sound somewhere between a gasp and a growl. From where she stood, his eyes looked almost black. But he didn't seem scared. He had the same look on his face as when he was cornered in Jez's kitchen. Wild, furious, unrestrained. Lees' stomach dropped.

"Hiya, boss!" Lees practically shouted as she continued toward the group. Two other workers stepped sideways to intercept her. She recognized one of them as Eria's unofficial right-hand man. Both reeked of liquor as they leaned over her. She ignored both and caught Eria's eye between their swaying bodies. "Ah, I see you got to the new bug before I had a chance."

"What's it to ya, Lice?" Eria barked. He pressed his weight further into Meshi but kept his eyes on Lees. She took a deep breath in an attempt to slow her racing heartbeat, willing her voice to remain steady.

"Came in with him. Got him talking up top, and he told me he's worth quite a bit of money," Lees replied.

"Is that so?" Eria grinned and turned back to Meshi.

"Wh-how dare you!" Meshi snarled. Eria flexed, and Meshi choked on whatever he was going to say next.

"Figured I had to get him quick. Rich mites don't stay in the mines very long, you know that," Lees continued. "A mite like me, from the Quarters? Nobody cares what happens to me. But a high family kid?" Lees gave a low whistle and patted one of the miners' shoulders. "Well. This one got a burly bodyguard topside, so someone must care what happens to him. Wonder what he'll do when his little lad comes back all bruised up? Or not at all? It's not like he can go back to the kid's family empty-handed without reporting at least a little revenge."

Eria's eyes narrowed as he took in Lees' words. He looked from Lees to the satchel Meshi clutched, then at the clothes he wore beneath the ill-fitting harness. Lees watched the foreman's resolve trickle away. He loosened his grip on the boy's neck.

"What's that matter?" One of his cronies barked. Lees ignored him.

"Let her go," Eria said. He stepped back from the wall, and Meshi crumpled to the ground.

"What're you doing, boss?"

"Don't need that kind of heat on me," Eria snapped. He jerked his head, and the two miners shuffled toward him. Before walking away, the foreman jabbed his finger at Lees and hissed, "You two better work until you dig up a pile of Hyper as tall as me."

Lees waited until they were out of view before rushing over to Meshi. He sat propped up against the wall, one hand still clutching that satchel and the other massaging his neck.

He hurriedly gathered the equipment he'd dropped in the altercation and mumbled, "Thanks."

"Don't thank me. Stop getting yourself into situations where I have to help you. You're going to have to learn how to fend for yourself down here," Lees scoffed. She consulted the slip of paper with their assignment again, then wordlessly beckoned him to follow her down the shaft.

Meshi didn't speak as they walked. Lees' frustration rose and fell with each footstep. She shouldn't be here. She wasn't on duty, and she wasn't getting paid. She shouldn't be here, but something in her chest pulled at her as if drawing her towards this pathetic, entitled highborn.

Not pathetic, Lees told herself. That wasn't quite the right word. It wasn't fair.

No, this wasn't like the feeling of needing to save a hurt, soft animal. This feeling of protectiveness was unshakeable, inexplicable.

Is this what I was like?

Her brain shouted *NO* out of indignation, but hadn't she been just like him not so long ago? When she first stepped off that train in Last Light, there hadn't been anyone to chaperone her through the town. She'd taken one step onto the platform and froze. The chippers shoved her forward, and she nearly fell over, watching any hope of returning home screech back up the train tracks. Lees was terrified. Broken. Alone.

Nobody wanted to be down here. Certainly not a mite, who didn't even know here was their fate until they arrived. This unwanted kinship had to be what she felt, right?

Lees pulled herself from the confusing swirl of thoughts and finally turned to look at Meshi. That tug in her chest tightened as her eyes trailed down to the bag he still held tightly against him, as if afraid now that Eria or someone else might sneak up and snatch it away.

"You should've just handed that over. Nothing's worth getting thrashed and left for dead down here."

Meshi's grip tightened almost imperceptibly.

"I'm not joking. People get hurt down here. People die. You need to be smarter about this stuff."

Meshi's eyes bore holes into her. He looked as though he was weighing his options, as if an important decision depended on the moment. Lees shifted away from him.

What the hell is that about?

Meshi peered over his shoulder in such an exaggerated gesture that Lees almost laughed. He turned back, his face dead serious, and unzipped the bag. She caught a glint of brass or silver before he withdrew his closed fist.

"You're wrong. Nothing is more important than this. I can't lose it," Meshi whispered. He unfurled his hand and revealed a deep orange gemstone mounted in an intricate gold setting. The gemstone was looped on a delicate golden chain.

The hair on the back of her neck stood up as she stared at the necklace. This was undoubtedly the most expensive piece of jewelry in all of Last Light. Lees' chest swelled with emotion, overcome by its beauty. Even in the dim lighting of the shaft, the gemstone sparkled and shone brightly. She tilted her head side to side and watched the light dance off its surface. The effect was mesmerizing, and it was almost as if Lees could see reflections on its surface moving as gracefully as the light. Goosebumps prickled across her skin. Almost unconsciously, she reached toward the pendant.

Meshi quickly closed his fist around the stone. He looked alarmed.

"Uh, sorry," Lees stammered. Her head felt suddenly heavy, and a low rumble filled her ears momentarily. She shook her head at the sensation, then laughed. "You really are an idiot."

"I am not! This is important," Meshi said, clenching his fist harder around the gemstone. He shook the fist holding the necklace, and the golden chain dangling from his hand flew back and forth. "It's a family heirloom."

Lees opened her mouth to reply, but Meshi suddenly squealed in pain and wrenched open his fingers to drop the necklace.

"I- I think - it burned me!"

The moment the stone hit the ground, the area erupted in an eye-wateringly brilliant orange light. It bathed the duo and seemed to stretch the entire length of the corridor.

"What's going on up there?" Eria's voice boomed through the shaft.

Lees was transfixed again. The stone looked different in the orange light somehow, more alive. Those reflections she'd glimpsed on its surface before seemed more pronounced. As she leaned forward to try to make out the shapes, a wave of joy and excitement shot through her body. Confusion gave way to comfort and happiness as the competing thoughts swirled through her mind. Another wave ran through her, her mind flitting between images and sensations – the feel of the sweater her mother had knitted for her as a child, the burning taste of Teeg's spicy curry, the cooling rush of air coming out of the tunnels, the smell of Jez's perfume – and Lees realized she had edged closer to the necklace. She wanted to reach for it, to touch it, to hold it close to her.

Meshi dove to the ground and jostled Lees to the side. Just as he reached out to snatch the necklace, it shook and jumped on its own, then rocketed down the mineshaft. The blinding orange light tracked its path as it zipped past Eria, who had just come up the incline.

"HEY!" He screamed, shielding his face. The necklace – visible only as a bright orange light – cascaded down the shaft and out of sight.

Lees and Meshi locked eyes. Without saying a word, they both decoupled their drills and chisels, Meshi throwing them to the ground and Lees gently setting hers down, before bolting down the tunnel after the necklace.

The duo bounded through the busy tunnel, dodging other miners and their carts.

"You're headed the wrong way, that area's not marked yet!" One of the miners yelled after Lees as the two raced past him. Lees barely heard him. The pendant's light was growing dimmer by the second. *Faster. Faster!*

Lees was bewildered, but the feeling took a backseat to the more urgent directive. A voice in her head was shouting to follow it, to fight through the stitch in her side, ignore the chunks of rocks flying through the air as the other workers drilled around them. Her vision narrowed. Nothing mattered but catching up to this glowing gemstone.

Soon, it was just the two of them. No rail carts, tracks, or mounted lights had been installed in this unexplored section of the mine. The dark, dank, silent tunnel brought forth an equally urgent voice in her head that was screaming *danger! Danger!* She still had enough sense not to die sightless and crushed in an unused mine corridor.

Lees slowed just enough to grab at the utility belt around her waist. Her hand skated across the miniature pickaxe and worked her way around to the flash box hooked near her back. She clipped the box onto her overalls and twisted the dial. A tinny yellow light, sickly and dull compared to the necklace's shine, flickered on.

Meshi had managed to keep pace with her. She noticed he didn't even seem winded. He must be in better shape than she'd initially thought, but something felt off. She'd watched him struggle to move and fight earlier today.

"Why'd you slow down? It's getting away," Meshi asked. All traces of aloofness gone. The edges of his words were more rounded now, as if his accent had somehow eroded.

"Are you playing some kind of trick on me?" Lees asked, pushing ahead of him as the tunnel narrowed.

"Why would I be playing a trick?"

"You're clearly a shaper pretending to be a mite," She

snapped. Meshi hesitated. Lees couldn't tell if he was hesitating because she'd clocked the lie correctly or if he was listening for the sound of the necklace bouncing off something ahead. His jaw flexed as the necklace clattered to the ground just at the edge of her lightbox's dim light, then dove to the right out of sight again.

"To what end?" Meshi argued, breaking their moment of silence. He tried to sidestep her, but Lees slammed her hand flat against his chest.

"I think this is a natural cave."

"So?" Meshi said, trying to push past her again.

"No, look, the drilling team kept moving straight and down," She pointed at the larger path ahead of them. "Miners don't make this smaller branch. They must have found it during the initial dig."

"Why does that matter?" Meshi asked impatiently. The necklace's light was fading down that side corridor. He made an exasperated sound before shoving her to the side and darting ahead.

Lees instinctively grabbed the back of his harness and spun him around. "Listen to me. We have no idea what's down there. If we get hurt or fall or stuck, nobody will come after us. Nobody is going to find us."

Meshi gently pried Lees' grip from his harness, stepped backward, and then ducked into the cave.

"Are you even listening to me!?" Lees called. No response. She shifted her weight from one foot to the other. The orange light was barely visible, and the voice screaming at her to follow drowned out the other, more rational one. Lees pulled out a small piece of chalk and drew a circle with a downward arrow cutting through it on the shaft wall before following Meshi into the cave.

Lees noticed the change instantly. The air felt thicker here, and the walls and ground were far slicker than the mineshaft. Her foot slipped almost immediately, but the rock wall was too slippery to steady herself. She fell and slid down a gentle incline on her butt. Her feet connected with Meshi's back at the bottom, and she smiled in grim satisfaction at his yelp of pain.

Her hand slipped on the ground beneath her, and she momentarily gave up on trying to stand. They both sat there and watched the orange light bound around the irregular corridor of the cave as it made its way further in.

Why had he stopped? Was he waiting for her? Lees wondered.

Meshi finally cleared his throat and awkwardly scrambled to his feet. He held out a hand to steady her as she did the same. One leg slipped, and she stopped short of doing the splits.

"It seems to be bouncing off solid ground as it goes, so that's good. No unexpected drops," Meshi said, somewhat sheepishly.

"We have to go back," Lees insisted.

"Why would we do that?" Meshi asked. He looked at her,

genuinely confused, then pointed to the bouncing light ahead of them. "I'm not the one doing that, I swear. Aren't you curious about what it is, though?"

Lees didn't know Meshi well enough. Was he just an exceptional liar? Was he a thief? Was he trying to lead her into a trap? What he was saying seemed impossible.

However, Lees couldn't help but think.

Meshi's name was on the mining roster. He was at least registered as a mite. If he really wasn't a shaper, that would mean this gemstone truly was moving on its own. Either he was working with a shaper to concoct an elaborate plan to rob her of a pair of half-decent work boots and some dust in her pockets, or...

Or what?

"Fine," Lees said through gritted teeth. "But you're walking first. I deserve better than to die falling down a hole to the center of the planet."

Meshi smiled broadly and nodded, then turned to follow the light.

Lees kept one hand on her pickaxe as they walked. The pull in her chest was almost an ache now, but something still didn't feel quite right. The weak light from her light box illuminated just enough of this natural cave to let her know they were too deep for help to arrive in time.

CHAPTER 5

Lees' Calling

Losing track of time down in the mines wasn't unusual, but the pair had been following the light for so long that Lees wondered if they'd stayed past their shift end. It could have been a few hours, it could have been the full 10 hours. The light had slowed enough for them to keep a steady walking pace, the bobbing orange pendant always staying just out of reach. Lees tried keeping track of their distance at first as a safety measure, but reluctantly gave up after second-guessing her pacing. She'd be way off base if she were counting too quickly, but even having that thought threw off the whole count. Try as she might to stay focused, Lees' concentration was slipping.

"Have you ever wondered how long a second is?" Lees

asked, breaking the silence for the first time since she'd agreed to follow him.

"What? No, can't say I have..." Meshi trailed off. Lees suspected he wasn't actually thinking about her question and decided against asking a follow-up one.

A second per footstep, a foot per step, but wouldn't my stride be more than someone else's? Numbers swirled in Lees' head, refusing to come together in a discernible formula.

Lees was too lost in thought to notice Meshi had stopped, and she smacked into his back. Something jagged in his duffel bag dug into her ribs. He lurched forward but kept his eyes locked on the corridor ahead. The necklace's orange light had stopped several dozen feet ahead of them. He crept forward slowly, as if approaching a skittish animal, then broke into a full sprint. Just as his hands stretched out to snatch it off the ground, Lees caught up to him, and the necklace jolted back to life. It bounded wildly around the passageway before shooting straight upwards, faster than before, the light fading into the darkness.

"Is that thing taunting us?" Lees asked breathlessly.

"We have to be close now," Meshi whispered. Lees stared at him, but he didn't elaborate. He started walking again without looking at her, but Lees paused, watching him creep forward into the darkness.

What isn't he telling me? Lees wondered.

"Ow!" Meshi shouted, then turned back to growl, "Can you *please* bring the light over here?"

Lees hid a smile before trotting over. Meshi stood a few inches back from a sheer wall, angrily rubbing his nose. As soon as the light hit the wall, Meshi's fingers scrabbled against the lumpy and irregular stone. The orange light had faded entirely somewhere beyond this wall, causing his search to become more desperate.

"It went up, then down," Lees said. Colder air pooled over them, and Lees looked up in alarm. The ceiling of stalactites and damp rock of the tunnel had vanished. Her light box illuminated the area immediately around them, but the darkness above them swallowed the weak beam.

She tried not to think about how far away they were from Last Light.

Lees shouldered past Meshi, who was now crouching to feel around the tunnel's edges. Lees stood on her tiptoes and ran her palms along the top of the tunnel. At the very height of her reach, with her arms extended as far as possible, her fingers curled over and felt nothing. She wiggled her fingers in the emptiness beyond the stone.

"It's a lip," She said, straining to feel beyond the edge. "The stone must have bounced up and beyond... well, whatever's on the other side."

Her eyes unfocused to conjure a mental image of what her hands were feeling, mapping out the possibilities. *Was this just an unusual wall formation in the middle of a tunnel that had partially collapsed, or did it lead into a larger chamber in the cave?*

Meshi pushed forward, and Lees' stomach dropped at the jostling. She teetered off balance and stumbled back, nearly tripping over his foot. Lees grabbed the back of his harness and yanked him away from the wall. She jabbed a finger in his chest and glared at him, noting with satisfaction that the lightbox on her shoulder was partially blinding him. Meshi threw up a hand to block the light, and Lees jabbed his chest again.

"Back off me, soft hands, or we're going to have a real problem," She snapped. "Do you know how dangerous natural caves are?"

"It's *my* necklace. I won't let you take it from me," Meshi sneered.

"I don't want your stupid necklace!" Lees said. *But is that a lie? There's something about it, but would I really steal it?* An image of the multifaceted gem glowing brightly danced across her vision. The aching pull in her chest surged almost painfully. She released his harness, exalted deeply, and gestured at the wall. "There seems to be an opening here. This wall doesn't extend all the way up."

Meshi felt along the wall to reach it, but he was shorter than Lees.

"Push me up," He demanded.

"Oh, absolutely not," Lees protested. "That could be a straight drop off on the other side." She scanned the cave opening above them and the yawning darkness beyond before continuing. "I'm not pushing you to your death. We need to go get a long rope, or better yet, bring a crew back with us."

"No," Meshi replied. Without pausing, he took a running start toward the wall and kicked off hard, hands scrambling to reach up and up, just managing to latch onto the lip. Using the uneven wall to gain purchase, he pulled himself awkwardly over the edge. Lees rushed forward to stop him and locked onto his legs. She wrapped herself around his knees and tried to think heavy thoughts to pull him back.

"Let - me - go!" He shouted. "I can see it! It's just - there - *let go!*"

"Do you have a death wish, you idiot?" Lees shouted back. She braced herself against the wall but was losing ground. Even with her full dead weight pulling him down, he was pulling her up, inch by painful inch.

"How are you this strong?" Lees groaned.

Meshi was doubled over the wall now and using his weight to pull her up with him. Gravity won in the end, their combined inertia pulling them violently over the wall. The pair fell fast and hard. Lees' and Meshi's screams bounced around them as they tumbled down, separating somewhere along the way down the fifty-foot slope. Lees was very aware of the blood rushing to her head from this angle. Sharp edges jabbed at Lees' shoulders and elbows as she struggled to flip around, every bump threatening to snap her neck. She tucked her knees and managed to orient herself feet-first, then saw stars as her chin slammed against another rock along the slope. Lees was skidding on her stomach now and felt one of the buckles on her harness snap. Bile crept up her throat and mingled with the taste of blood and grit. She couldn't stop. There was nothing to do as her body spun again in a bounce that rearranged her internal organs. Stone scraped every inch of her exposed skin as she skidded to the bottom of the bowl. Lees rolled over a few times before coming to a stop on her back.

Safety training kicked in again, and Lees carefully checked herself. Head, face, throat, chest, stomach, legs, fingers, toes... Her heart raced beneath her fingers, but she was more or less intact.

Satisfied that she wasn't bleeding out, Lees wrenched her eyes open and stared in awe. The massive chamber around them was alive. Brilliant shapes of every color imaginable twisted and spread across the cave walls and ceiling hundreds of feet above her. Ribbons of dazzling blues, reds, and yellows intersected and twisted, crashing into each other before separating just as quickly.

So enthralled with the sight, Lees hadn't even bothered trying to count how long she sat like that. A soft groan somewhere to her left pulled her out of the trance, and she slowly sat up. Lights exploded across her eyes, and a wave of nausea rolled over her. She waited for it to end, breathing in through her nose and looking around to keep herself from barfing. From here, she could see even thicker bands of colors wrapped around jutting stone shapes all along the walls and floor of this huge cavern.

Meshi was struggling to roll over. A few strings of greens and pinks rolled beneath him, illuminating the shape of his body from below. Lees looked around and noticed other natural entry points speckled along the cave, including a vast pit of darkness just beyond the thin plateau she and Meshi sat on. Lees swallowed painfully at the sight and glanced back at Meshi, who grimaced and turned his face away. She reached over and turned off the now pointless light box that had once again blinded him.

Lees' head cleared. With eyes mostly adjusted to the light and her stomach contents firmly in place, her attention snapped to the platform they were on. *How thick was this stone? How safe were they?* The rock beneath them was smooth and flat, almost unnaturally so. She placed an open palm to the smooth surface and noticed it was warm to the touch. Thin tendrils of purple light twisted up and around her fingers, appearing to almost lift off the ground to drift along her skin before continuing their journey on.

The purple light raced toward the center of the room, as all the other veins seemed to do. Her eyes traced its path and finally saw what the lights were rushing toward. At the tip of the plateau stood a large stone sphere, its surface worn smooth from a steady stream of water falling from high above the cave. The water pooled at the top and ran down the sides of the plateau and far below. Lees was struck by the serenity of this strange natural water feature, its surface sparkling as multicolored lights shimmered through the water.

Something blocked her view, and she looked up in alarm. Her less-than-favorable companion's frame towered over her. Lees blinked at him and watched Meshi touch something wet on his face. He scowled as he realized it was blood, a souvenir from their tumble over the wall.

"You happy? I got cut thanks to your flailing," He spat.

"You're still breathing, aren't you?" Lees retorted.

Meshi's head snapped to the side at a tiny but persistent sound in the distance. Their lovely little guide was repeatedly clanging against the central stone sphere now, smacking into it, bouncing off, then speeding back toward it again and again. Lees hadn't even noticed it before. The pendant's orange shine seemed much duller against this cavern's glow, and the rushing water from above almost completely drowned out the sound of its assault.

Without a word, Meshi darted in its direction.

"Oh, yeah, sure. *'Thanks for your help, Lees, I'd be crushed upside down in a hole without you here to guide me,'*" Lees muttered.

Up close, the stone sphere was massive, rivaling that of Teeg's two-story shop. Lees walked a few paces behind Meshi, drawn forward by the pendant's attempt to break through the sphere's almost crystalline exterior.

"What could have made this?" Lees wondered. Meshi didn't respond, instead running his hand along the rough stone side of the sphere and sliding his hand into a water-worn divot. The pendant clanged away above them, but he paid it no attention now.

Lees reached up and looped her finger through the chain before gently pulling the pendant away from the stone. It struggled weakly against her before rebounding straight into her palm. She pinched the stone between her fingers almost on instinct, and the weak ache in her chest exploded out across her body. She gasped at the pain that tore at her, a pain not physical but of something more profound. Lone-liness, cold and empty, and loss, sharp and persistent.

And then the feeling faded just as suddenly.

She turned the stone over in her hand and noticed just how bright it was compared to the dim yellow Hyper dust she mined every day. Real gold ringed the pendant, and the finely looped chain was so intricately woven that Lees couldn't help but wonder who could be skilled enough to shape something like this.

"I think we can break this open!" Meshi called from the other side of the sphere.

"Wait, what?" Lees snapped back to reality. The dazzling light display was incredible, absolutely astonishing once-in-a-lifetime type stuff, but this wasn't a dream. They were potentially miles below Last Light, hours away from the fore-man and their team, and without supplies to last more than a day or two. Sure, it was weird that the necklace was moving on its own, but there was no way Lees was going to die for a mystery.

"It doesn't seem that thick. The water has eroded a lot of it away, so we don't need to get through much," Meshi continued.

"Are you kidding? We have no idea what this thing is made of," Lees said.

"Yes we do," Meshi said as he rounded back towards Lees. "It's clearly *Hyper* dust."

"Yes, clearly, of course this massive sphere is pure Hyper," Lees replied. "So says the mite who's only been in the mines for less than a day. You have no idea what's inside this sphere. It could be gas or even some kind of incendiary material lying in wait to blow us into a thousand pieces."

Meshi glared at her and noticed the necklace in her hand. He held out his own and wiggled his fingers before saying slowly, "It's mine, remember?"

Lees slapped the necklace back into his hand, then jabbed a finger at him again.

"No, we don't go around breaking open strange stones. If we get out of here – *if* – we wait to get a crew down here to inspect it. Then *maybe* we crack it open."

Lees craned her neck to look up the slope they'd fallen down. *Could we scale it with pickaxe alone? Would that give us enough grip?* She started to unclip items from her belt, feeling an uncharacteristic lightness on her side, when –

CLAAANG!

The sound of a pickaxe hitting stone echoed through the massive cavern. Frustration boiled over, tightening Lees' chest and rushing up her neck. She whipped around to see Meshi peering into a tiny fissure he'd made in the stone with *her pickaxe*. He lifted *her pickaxe* and arced it backward with a clumsy grip.

Lees flew across the distance between them and grabbed the pickaxe as it reached its apex. Meshi jolted off balance and fell onto his back. Lees leaned over him now, gripping the pickaxe menacingly.

"You *idiot*. You absolute fuckass piece of ungrateful shit. I protect you from being beaten black and blue, get dragged back into the mine without pay because of you, and I follow you and this stupid glowing necklace down an uncharted drift for hours. I keep you safe, I'm nice to you, and this is what I get in return?" Lees shouted. Her own voice echoed in her ears, partially drowned out by a persistent ringing sound. She threaded her hands through his lapels, pulled him to his feet, and slammed him against the sphere. His head bounced against the stone with a thwack. He clamped onto her wrists, trying to wrestle her away. The golden chain of the necklace grazed her forearm, and the pendant bumped against her hand as he struggled.

White-hot rage coursed through Lees' veins, and she

repeated the gesture while cursing through gritted teeth, "You are an entitled, spoiled, soft, helpless child who got everything handed to him and can't stand the idea of not getting his way."

"Stop, stop, let me go!" Meshi begged. He wasn't focused on her, even as she smashed him against the sphere. "It's here – I know it's here. *Let go!*"

"No!" Lees snapped. "Not until you listen to me and admit you don't know everything. You're just a mite like the rest of us, with a shitty attitude and a fancy necklace."

Meshi looked nervous now. He tightened his grip on her wrists, and a panicked, reckless look flashed across his eyes. Lees recognized the look. With a final burst of anger, Lees drew him back and slammed him into the sphere again. A crack splintered across its surface on impact, splitting it almost perfectly in half. She let go of Meshi more out of shock than malice, and the boy slammed backward into the hollowed sphere.

Lees froze, not sure what to expect. To her astonishment and relief, no hazardous gas, liquid, or even creepy crawly emerged from the gaping hole. The necklace in Meshi's hand yanked wildly, snapping against the chain over and over again, like a dog tied to a leash.

"What did you do!?" Meshi screeched.

She didn't respond and instead stepped over him into the shattered sphere.

"Huh, you were right," Lees muttered, her anger dissipating.

The sphere's interior was made entirely of hardened, crystallized Hyper dust. Its violent swirling pattern of brilliant light was disorienting – she'd never seen anything so terrifying and beautiful. The jagged shapes pulled and rolled over one another, forming eerie tendrils that strained to reach the sphere's center.

It took a few moments for Lees' eyes to make out the shape amid the flashing and crashing lights. But there, resting atop a thin pedestal of chaotically hardened dust, was a star-shaped, blood-red stone. It was small, tiny even, no bigger than the diameter of a carrot, its surface covered in dozens of rounded points. The moment her eyes fixed on it, truly seeing it amid the swirling explosions around her, it lit up with a flash that emitted such a bright light that it drowned out everything else and bathed the entire cavern in red.

She had to squint to keep her eyes open. The light that danced across the surface of every facet and divot of this stone wasn't reflecting from another source but from within it somehow. The hardened Hyper dust shone in a thousand different ways, erupting with countless shapes and patterns.

It was painful to look at, but Lees didn't turn away. She couldn't.

The air left Lees' lungs as she looked at the star-shaped object. Its light filled her mind and swirled around her thoughts, bathing even her insides with its crimson light. And it was comforting, a warm embrace, a welcome presence.

The world around her fell away. She barely noticed. Until the dazzling lights abruptly shattered, giving way to a deep darkness. An enormous shape appeared, a disembodied, crystallized hand of a giant held tight in a fist. A scream rose in Lees' chest but died before it reached her throat. The impossibly enormous hand opened to reveal the star-shaped object floating in its palm.

That pull again – the ache in her chest – intensified, as if beckoning her forward to take the object. But Lees hesitated, taking a step back.

Hyper dust crumbled under her weight, and Lees felt the heel of her foot dip down. A quick glance down, and fear shot through her body. She stood at the edge of a flat crystal platform, her weight teetering enough to coat her back in a thin sheen of panicked sweat. Lees threw herself forward, away from the edge, but there was nowhere else to turn.

"Let me go," She demanded, summoning any dredge of bravery remaining in her. The giant hand did not move.

"I don't want it," Lees lied. "What have you done with Meshi?" Again, the hand did not move. "The boy who was with me—don't hurt him."

Two fingers on the enormous hand twitched, and the others curled inward almost imperceptibly. Then it reached out towards her again, tilting the palm down to beckon Lees to grab the stone.

She tried not to look at it, but the ache in her chest felt like it was escaping her ribcage. Desire consumed her like she'd never felt before, not for her favorite meal, or Jez's embrace, or revenge on the chippers who dragged her from her home. She had never wanted anything more than this in her entire life, Lees was sure of it.

Whatever brittle willpower she had left snapped. Lees reached for the stone slowly, tentatively. Her fingers hovered over it, and electricity radiated through her palm and up her arm, leaving tingling goosebumps in its wake. Her mind raced with images of the blood-red stone's shifting plasma-like form. She saw herself holding it high above her head until the red light consumed Last Light. Thousands of eyes peered at her from the darkness, tendrils reaching out to tear at her flesh, to pull her into their writhing mass.

Lees' stomach flipped, her breath caught in her throat, and she jerked her hand back. Even if she had to jump, she would escape – but the electricity of the stone held her fast, as if her hand were a magnet drawn to it. The giant crystal hand was a deeper, richer color now. It reached out to grab her, the fingers spreading to encompass her body easily, and the star-shaped stone's points shot out in all directions to pierce her and the walls of the black void.

She screamed as the stone twisted and shifted, her skin ripping against the spikes spinning wildly. The crystal hand reached for her, to squeeze, to destroy—and suddenly the vision vanished.

Lees was back on the plateau, standing in the now darkened, shattered sphere. Sweat matted her hair and dripped down her face, and one hand was outstretched over the Hyper dust pedestal. She was whole, unharmed, but the stone was gone – and so was Meshi.

CHAPTER 6

The Hyper Object

Lees bolted back out into the cavern. The multicolored swirls flashing around her now seemed dim compared to the light she sought. Her eyes snapped to the right – there! Brilliant red bounced around as Meshi sprinted toward the cave wall with the stone clenched in his hand.

She moved to follow, but her vision blurred as new images raced through her mind. Meshi standing over her, striking her again and again with her own hand axe. Meshi's blood-splattered face grimacing with the effort. The stone pressed tightly between the palm of his left hand as he raised the sanded-smooth shaft of the axe above his head with the other. Shards of pure-white bone – her rib cage, a tibia, a tooth – flying as he swung.

The details were so vivid that when Lees tripped forward, she grabbed at her chest to staunch the bleeding.

Meshi grunting while rolling her limp and battered body over the edge of the plateau and down into the endless abyss below.

Lees' stomach flipped, and she shook her head, eyes squeezed shut. The cavern came back into focus, lit up with a rainbow of colors, none of which were her own bodily fluids. Another wave of nausea rolled over her. *How could I even see myself like that? What's wrong with me?*

The swishing of an axe launched Lees to her feet, but the sound was too far away to be a threat. Meshi was clawing up the stone wall, working the axe into its cracks as he went. She quickly closed the distance between them. With one swift move, Lees yanked the scrawny boy from the wall by the back of his jumpsuit and threw him to the ground.

"Were you just going to leave me here!?" She screamed.

Meshi wriggled on the ground before pulling himself upright. When he turned toward her, Lees took a step back. His body went rigid, his face now a snarling mask of fury.

"You were trying to take what belonged to me!" He growled. His voice had dipped a few pitches, and Lees leaned away. This wasn't the crazed look of a cornered animal she'd seen in the kitchen. This was something more.

Could he be seeing those visions too? Is that why he's acting like this? Lees wondered in alarm.

An image of Meshi, his body warped and twisted,

snatching a loaf of bread from the Eye of Mite's kitchen, flashed before her.

A loaf of bread?

Another image of Meshi, his features exaggerated, reaching for her beloved drill and absconding with it. Her jaw tensed involuntarily. *That thief!*

"Hang on," Lees muttered. She shook her head again, exacerbating the headache creeping across the top of her skull. "I don't think this thing is safe. It's messing with our minds."

Meshi stretched his mouth wide to show his teeth and pressed his fist holding the stone to his chest.

"Meshi, listen to me. Give me the stone. We have to get rid of it, it's –" Lees snapped her mouth shut.

There was something wrong with this kid, had been wrong since before they entered the mine. She didn't even know him. What if he wasn't seeing any visions? What if he truly planned to leave her here, or turn her in for seeing things once they got to the surface? What if –

"Aha! You *are* trying to steal it from me!" Meshi's suddenly high-pitched laugh echoed around them. His pupils were enormous when he glared at her again. "I won't let you have it!"

Still holding the stone in one hand, Meshi lunged at Lees with the hand axe. He swung it in a wavering arc, trying to force her back. But he was off balance, and Lees had faced much more capable fighters in her short time at Last Light.

Lees leaned back, waited for the arcing weapon to pass her, and then launched herself at him. He sluggishly whipped the axe backwards, but Lees was faster. When she slammed him to the ground, his grip loosened, and the hand axe clattered away and fell into the chasm.

Meshi clawed at her clothes, desperately trying to push her off with his one free hand. What he lacked in expertise, he made up for in desperation. His nails dug into her cheek, tearing two long stripes into her skin and ripping his own nail off in the process. Meshi howled in pain and anger. Lees registered the dull sting, but it felt distant somehow. A fresh burst of adrenaline-fueled energy spurred her movements. She pinned his arms down with her knees and grabbed his wrist.

Flashes of colors illuminated their struggle. Lees dug her thumbs into his wrist and palm to pry his hand open. Meshi tried to buck her off with his legs and hips.

This has *to be from the stone,* Lees thought.

"No! Stop it, you can't take this from me. It's supposed to belong to me!" Meshi yelled over and over. Saliva flew from his mouth as he whipped his head around, flailing every free inch of his body against her.

"Sorry," Lees whispered. She dug her nails into his palm and tore at his fingers, leaning her full weight into the knee on his forearm. He snapped his teeth at her face, barely missing her ear when she jerked away. With a final tug, Lees prised the stone from the boy's grip and rolled forward away from him.

Lees didn't feel her forehead bang against the ground. The moment she touched the stone, darkness consumed her. Meshi was gone. Instead, her knees smacked down on the unnaturally smooth surface of the black void floor.

The crystal hand had found her again. It loomed from the emptiness around her, slithering through the air with its approach. The hand no longer reached out but squeezed into a fist, poised to strike at her. The stone throbbed in her hand like a miniature heartbeat, thrumming just as erratically as her own.

Lees threw herself backwards and scrambled away, barely dodging the hand as it slammed into the ground. The fist burst open. Crystalized fingers towered over her, splayed to form a cage around her, and lunged. It was impossibly fast.

"GET AWAY FROM ME!" Lees shrieked. Closer, so close, inches from crushing her – but at the sound of her voice, the hand twitched and froze.

Her arm yanked forward, the force of it tearing at her shoulder socket and causing her to tumble forward and fall flat on her stomach with her arm outstretched. Red sand pooled around her wrist and clenched fist, squeezing and bashing her hand against the hard stone.

"*L-E-T G-O!*" A distant, straining voice pierced through her mind. Its familiar, clipped whining parted the fog of pain long enough for Lees to orient herself. The throbbing in her hand, frantic to the point of almost vibrating, brought her back to her senses.

"No!" Lees whispered. She got to her knees and pulled back on her arm. Retching it from the hold of the crystal – from Meshi. She still couldn't see what was happening to her beyond the oppressive blackness of the room, but his intentions were clear.

"It's too dangerous!" She shouted, for all the good it did. Lees didn't need the fresh wave of visions of her and Meshi plummeting to their deaths fighting over the stone to understand what would happen if she didn't get rid of this thing.

Every muscle in her shoulder screamed as her arm yanked forward again, but Lees forced herself to shove the pain down. Rather than pulling away, she leapt forward, knocking the invisible assailant over.

There was a momentary reprieve. Lees reared back and caught sight of the crystal hand one more time. The enormous fingers struggled as if held by invisible restraints. She lunged with one foot forward and threw the stone as far from her as possible. Her vision cleared instantly. Meshi came into focus, red-faced and wild hair, roaring in frustration as the stone sailed over his head. They both watched the stone arc past the sphere and down into the darkness, clattering once against the wet walls before falling deeper and deeper into its depths. Meshi launched himself after it, careening toward the edge and abyss below without hesitation. Lees threw her arms around his legs and pulled with her full weight. Meshi crashed to the ground, one arm still outstretched. The red light had already faded to nothing.

All was silent save for the pair's irregular panting. Lees looked at Meshi. His gaze was fixed on the spot where the red stone disappeared. She stared at the back of his head for a moment, willing herself to think beyond the pain pulsating across her body.

"The stone. I felt – it's like it took over my mind."

Meshi turned his face toward her, but his eyes remained on the spot just beyond the broken sphere. He nodded vaguely in her direction.

"Took over your mind. Huh," He shook his head and slowly stood up. "Yeah. Mine too..."

Lees could almost see flashes of the object in her mind, like trying to recall a vivid dream, as if it was still somehow calling out to her. Shadows and dripping water and an endless spiraling down, down, down. The visions faded to scraps of thought, then to echoes.

When she took stock of herself this time, Lees was in worse condition than when they'd fallen into the cavern. Her knuckles were bleeding. Dark purple bruises had already formed on her forearms.

Meshi watched her feel the lump on her cheek. Her eyes darted to meet his, and he swallowed.

"I'm, uh, I don't know what to say. I don't know what came over me. It's like, I wanted to, uh," Meshi eyed Lees. She could practically feel him cataloging every tool on her harness and jumpsuit. He looked away, then mumbled, "It made me want to attack you."

At least it wasn't just me, Lees thought, her spirits buoying slightly despite herself.

"What was that thing?" Lees asked.

All bravado and rage were gone when Meshi looked at Lees this time. He opened and closed his mouth a few times. Lees imagined him as a monk fish out of water, big mouth gasping for air – *do I have a concussion?* – before snapping back to reality.

"I believe..." Meshi started slowly. He closed his eyes, then finished in a rush, "I think that was the Hyper Object. It was thought to be lost, buried deep in the planet or destroyed somehow, but – well, you saw it. That's what it was. It's here."

Lees erupted in laughter. It was a deep, cackling laughter that pulled at her sore insides.

"The Hyper Object!? Like, in the folk tale?" She wheezed. Laughter turned to giggling, then dissolved into coughing that tasted metallic.

Meshi's face remained stony.

"Oh, c'mon. There's no way that thing actually exists," She snorted.

Except...

She ran through the last hour in her head, the moments leading from one impossible vision to the next. Glimpses of the future. A place out of time and space. Otherworldly pain. Flashing lights, crystallized shapes. Could it be?

"Oh, it very much exists, and we almost killed each other over it," Meshi assured her, his voice taking a hardened edge. Lees found herself wondering how old this kid really was.

Meshi began pacing, turning to look over the edge of the plateau at each pass.

"The Hyper Object was stolen from the high families hundreds of years ago by a misguided Seer – and then they lost the damn thing!" Meshi ranted. He gestured at the cavern around them. "What a fool to get buried all the way down here."

"Did you say a see-er? What does that mean?" Lees asked.

"Do they teach you nothing this far underground?" Meshi exclaimed. Lees glared at him. "Sorry, sorry. Suppose most people haven't met one before. A Seer is what we call a shaper who can commune with Hyper. They're rare. They're still powerful without the Hyper Object, but with it... well, let's just say there's hardly anything more valuable to the Oppri."

Lees imagined herself holding the object again, with its many points prickling into her skin, but instead of itchy pain, she was awash in contentment. Warmth radiated from the spot she imagined embracing the stone, right in the center of her chest. *The high families. The Oppri.* Her head swam with the image of Teeg, Jez, her mother, the rest of her family, all clad in the finest linens, seated at a long table buckling under the weight of an enormous feast. Joined together for a meal more decadent than she could possibly imagine. A crowd of her favorite people smiling, laughing, pouring drinks

- healthy, clean, happy. Light sparkled across the gilded dining room, with the Crest visible from the open windows.

She smiled at the idea.

Her fantasy was rudely interrupted by a sharp whistling sound that grew louder and louder. Blood-red light streamed up from beyond the plateau.

Meshi's mouth dropped. The bright stone zoomed out from the cave's depths, its radiant light dancing off the cave walls as it rocketed toward the duo. Spiraling multicolored lights erupted along the surfaces around them as it passed. Then another sound drowned out the whistling – the walls around them crackled as Hyper dust and other minerals broke away to follow the object's path. The cavern became alive as if responding to the object.

Meshi barely had enough time to duck as the object flew past him into Lees' open hand. The force of it hitting her sent a shockwave out and almost knocked them both to the ground as the trailing Hyper showered down around them in a brilliant spectacle.

Darkness did not envelop Lees this time. No enormous crystal hand, no invisible threats, no visions. Though her brief fantasy was over, the warmth it conjured returned and settled in her chest.

"You called it back."

The words left Meshi's mouth without him realizing it, dripping with exhaustion and frustration and something Lees couldn't quite identify. Envy? Anger? Fear? But he backed up while Lees inspected the object. Still no visions, no crystal hand, just an unmoving stone in the palm of her hand.

"I think you were right. This thing is dangerous. You should get rid of it," He said, unsettled.

Lees tore her eyes away from the stone. Her heartbeat was returning to normal, and the pain was easing in her ribs and face. Calmness relaxed the tension in her muscles that she'd been clenching since they got here.

"I guess, but it seems different now."

Images of cold darkness tinged with desperate loneliness flashed across her mind. She stared down at the object, wondering. *Is it reacting to me? Is it trying to talk to me?*

Or is it a trap?

Lees threw the stone deep down the corridor. Meshi sucked air between his teeth and ducked down. Nothing happened. She absently traced the spot on her palm where it had been, remembering the now-gone calmness it seemed to bring. Maybe the feeling was just an aftereffect of the fantasy? The realization that the fight was over? It *had* felt nice, though. Why did it feel like there was a connection –

The little object flew right back into her hand before she had a chance to finish the thought. An unmistakable bloom of joy burst in her chest.

A warm breeze. The smell of chicory brewing on a cold morning. Her mother's knitted socks snug on her feet late at night. The comfort of an embrace, safe and quiet.

Lees rolled the object in her hand. *This thing is definitely communicating with me.* Something buzzed in her ear. She looked up to find Meshi staring at it hungrily again.

"I'm keeping it for now," Lees said loudly. She tucked the object into the front pocket in her satchel, then looped it through her belt. When the object faded from view, the cavern visibly darkened. The ribbons of Hyper veins around them ceased moving and lost their energy.

"Wait, no, you can't do that," Meshi said, as if coming out of a daze.

The cavern transformed until the only visible light came from the weak light box on Lees' shoulder. Lees' mind felt clearer despite the dark.

"We gotta move. Once we're out safe, clear minds can figure this out. For now, focus on climbing," Lees said. She pushed Meshi's shoulder to spin him around, and they both began trying to climb the sloped wall back into the corridor they'd come from. Without a hand axe or other tools, it was slow going – almost impossible – but Lees said nothing.

They struggled this way for a while until Meshi slid back down the slope and slumped against it. Lees tried to think about their predicament, but her mind kept returning to the vision of that feast with her family. The rich aroma of stewed meat, the sweet tang of vinium, the glow of the decorated chandelier over the table, throwing light around the room.

Wait, something *was* throwing light around the room. Cavern. Whatever.

"Oh, no," Meshi moaned, pointing at the light. But its

movement didn't have the erratic quality the multicolored Hyper veins had before. It was moving slowly, growing brighter, until suddenly a group of hard hats poked out from the edge above them.

"You okay, pipsqueak?" A familiar voice called out from above. It was Teeg.

Lees sparked to life, happy her hasty chalk directions and unexpected absence had led Teeg and his crew here.

"Yes! We're here! We're okay! But we're stuck," Lees shouted back. The pair stepped back, and a knotted rope ladder swung down from above.

Meshi grabbed Lees' arm when she reached for it. He stared at her with a hardened look and dropped his voice to a whisper. "Don't tell them anything about this. They won't understand."

She studied his face before gently pulling his hand off her, whispering, "Don't you think they need to know about this? What's here?"

"No!" Meshi growled, then collected himself with a sigh. "I can explain when we get back to town. Just – just promise not to say anything until we can talk to Ike." Lees gave him a blank look. "Ike, my bodyguard. The guy I came with? It'll make more sense. Trust me."

Trust you!? A voice screeched in her head at the very idea. How could she trust this entitled liar who lured her down here and tried to kill her under the influence of some object from a folk tale? She chewed her lip, a line forming between her eyes as she considered the proposal.

"You coming!?" Teeg shouted down to them.

That crystal hand had almost squeezed the life out of her. Meshi had almost ripped her arm off trying to take the stone from her. The stone had nearly cut a hole straight through his head as it flew into her hand.

What if this object took over her body? What if she hurt somebody? Another vision flashed across her eyes, this one originating not from the stone but from the darkest recesses of her mind: Teeg lying motionless on the floor while she stood over him, her body now covered in deadly red crystal.

Lees nodded curtly and tilted her head back to smile up at Teeg. "On our way!" She called.

She gripped the rope ladder and began to climb. As she ascended, she called again, "There's tons of Hyper in this room. Y'all should bring a crew to excavate it tomorrow."

Meshi struggled up the ladder behind her, but he was visibly relaxed. Lees would keep the secret, for now. She'd play nice and hear out this bodyguard to learn whatever she could about this mystery object. But then she was done listening to these strangers. She'd make her own decisions from there.

CHAPTER 7
Meshi's Intentions

Retracing their route through the natural drift and back into the mine proper took less time than Lees expected. She kept one hand over the front pocket of her pouch so her fingertips could graze the edges of the stone through the canvas. For some reason it felt safer to stay in contact with it, however indirect. Lees and Meshi allowed themselves to be shuttled to the main shaft and into the cage without protest. Teeg tried in vain to start a conversation with Lees, but gave up after the second attempt and settled against the railing in silence as they ascended.

When the pair exited the tunnel, they split off from the rescue crew and other workers, most of whom were still finishing their day's work before heading to Jez's saloon. Rather than joining them and spending the evening admiring Jez's work ethic, she waved off Teeg and motioned for Meshi to follow her up the carved steps back toward town. Based on the situation they'd left him in, she had a pretty good idea of where the boy's bodyguard might have ended up.

Meshi and Lees walked in complete silence. Lees had no idea what to say after what happened, let alone understand what Meshi was thinking.

Every thought seemed to turn back to the pulsating sensation emanating from the mysterious stone. She ran her fingers over the little lump in the pocket without thinking, then glanced at Meshi. He wasn't looking at her, didn't seem to notice. Meshi kept his eyes pinned to the ground as he dutifully followed her to their destination.

The doctor's office had been one of the first buildings constructed in Last Light. It was a squat square building made of cobblestone and mortar with slate tile accents. Early building methods and materials held strong throughout the years, none of that cheaply shaped clapboard or bent tin that held up most of the newer constructions. Like many buildings in Oppri, it had been built on a flat, open space with a short fence railing made of decorative cobblestone running along its perimeter.

As they approached the large wraparound front porch, Lees spotted Dr. Hayes reclining in a rocking chair and could smell the fragrant spiced tea he was sipping. Last Inn's doctor was a rail-thin man in his late 60s with wiry hair he kept cropped short. He wore oversized, round glasses and a long, heavy coat, regardless of the temperature. Lees liked Dr. Hayes just fine, but what she really loved was his companion. The man never went anywhere without his giant feline purt named Gripes.

They rounded the corner and were greeted by the sight of Gripes stretching her paws in a deep bow. Meshi hesitated on the first step as Gripes licked her fangs. This purt was taller than Lees on her hind legs and much faster than she could ever hope to be. Gripes had what Lees believed to be the most luxurious grey and white fur of any animal, which ran down her body and extended to the tip of her surprisingly swishy tail.

Lees leaned down to scratch behind her ears, but Meshi remained standing still on the same stair. "Hey, doc. Not sure if he's here, but we're here to see —"

"Room four," The reclining doctor drawled without looking up from his reading. Lees smirked and opened the door to head inside. Meshi hesitantly followed but kept his eyes on Gripes, who watched him closely as he passed.

"I hate purts..." Meshi groaned once safely on the other side of the door. Lees didn't respond.

Lees knocked on room four and slid the door open. Like most of the exam and recovery rooms in the building, this one was lined with complicated machines mostly made of iron and glass. Most of them were switched off, which meant the burly man wasn't in critical condition. She'd only ever seen the doctor treat one person on the verge of death, and the room was brighter than a thousand Rapidite nodes as every one of Dr. Hayes' machines rattled and churned and did whatever they were meant to do to keep people alive.

Sure, the place was a drain on Last Light's local power, but no mining town would last long without someone who could patch workers back up. Lees nearly snapped her arm in half her first week on the job, but Hayes got her back to work the next day, and she never again grumbled about the tax taken from her pay to subsidize the spinwheels' time to keep those generators running.

She stood in the doorway and let Meshi pass her into the room. The enormous bodyguard pushed himself up in the bed and collapsed against the headboard with a groan.

"Meshi, there you are," His voice sounded thin and raspy.

"How're you feeling, Ike?" Meshi asked. His tone rang hollow, as if distracted.

"M'okay now," Ike groaned with the effort of sitting up and shifted in the bed. His shoulders were so broad that he practically hung off either side of the narrow bedframe. The gauze-like blanket covering him fell away, and Lees could now see the bandage wrapped tightly across his stomach. She couldn't help but admire how physically fit this man was, though his arms and chest were decorated with scars of every shape and size.

"The knife only took a chunk out of me, but missed the important bits-"

"Good, yeah, okay," Meshi interrupted. Then he blurted, "So we found something, Ike." Lees' hand automatically moved to press against the stone still secured in her bag. Both men were staring at her now.

"Lees, it's okay. Just show him," Meshi said.

Ike winced and put his hand on his stomach, but otherwise remained still. Waiting. Lees unsnapped the pouch, releasing the red glow from the Hyper Object inside. She slowly reached in and felt the pulse of energy it emitted intensify. Ike's eyes widened when the light filled the room. An electrical shock raced through Lees' fingertips as they made contact with the sharp edges of the stone. Meshi leaned forward with his eyes fixed on Lees' hand in the pouch.

At its touch, Lees saw flashes of visions again. Knocking Meshi down, running before he even hit the ground, racing out the door and down the streets where she knew he wouldn't be able to follow, losing him in the alleys.

She jerked her hand back out of the pouch and shook her head to clear away the images. The red glow dimmed, then faded entirely as she sealed the pouch closed again.

"Did you see that?" Meshi cooed at Ike.

Ike didn't break eye contact with Lees.

"What did you see?" He asked in a low voice. Lees' eyes searched the room for anything other than Ike's gaze. Her stomach turned. She hated this, could feel his eyes boring into her, peeling her apart, ready to catch even the hint of a lie. The pressure. He waited. She caved.

"Is that what this object does?" Lees snapped. "Does it show you visions? Violence? Desires?"

She threw her hands out wide, disgust welling in her throat. "I didn't want it. I didn't want any of that. I threw it away – *twice*." Lees began pacing the room, eyes sliding along every weird machine she passed. "It came after us, it consumed our minds. I tried chucking it in the ravine, but even then it kept calling to me! I see what it wants... It wants horrible, horrible things. Wants me to do horrible things."

Meshi stepped forward to block Lees' path and reached out as if to comfort her.

"We knew the object would be dangerous, but I couldn't get you away from it," He said softly.

The words cut through Lees' mind like a knife. We knew. Lees jerked away from Meshi in shock, mouth agape. "What do you mean, you *knew!?*"

Meshi's eyes widened, and he looked toward Ike pleadingly. The bodyguard remained silent. He turned back to Lees, stuttering, "Well, Lees, listen. Yes, I know what I said, but the fact that it showed us both visions, I-I mean," He swallowed and his voice steadied. "It pushed us both to hurt each other. It's clearly dangerous. I knew we had to come here to contain it."

Meshi turned around, pulled his duffel bag onto a chair, and unzipped it. His voice shifted in pitch as he talked, now addressing her with an almost clinical tone as he fished around inside the bag. "I haven't been totally honest with you. We're from the Oppri. I'm a scholar, I told you that, but I'm specifically studying the Hyper Object. The sheer amount of Hyper this mine town produces led me to believe the object might have been here at one point. We might find traces of it to lead us to it. That's why we came."

Lees' face felt red hot. To her horror, her vision blurred as frustrated tears welled up in her eyes. She quickly wiped them away when she realized Ike was still watching her. He hadn't said a word. *Why was he just staring at me?*

Meshi held out a small box. It was made of flat green stone, shaped into a simple cube, and featured a fabricated toggle latch to hold the lid in place. "This box is made of pure Periax." Meshi studied Lees' face, waiting for confirmation. "We know-" he caught the murderous look on Lees' face and quickly corrected. "In our research, we've discovered that Periax has a dampening effect on Hyper. Once the object rests in here, it will no longer torment you. You can be free of this... chaos." As Meshi said the word, he winced in pain.

Is he still being affected by the object as well? Lees wondered. Even now, with the object turned away, hazy images that weren't her own played in the back of her mind. The object wanted her to listen to it, wanted to be seen. Was seeking attention.

But why? Why her? Mites don't have any connection to Hyper. That was their big failure, their biggest flaw. Her own grandmother had wasted years trying to train her, and nothing came of it. She couldn't move it, couldn't will it to act on her behalf, couldn't interact with Hyper at all. So why the hell was this damn rock trying so hard to talk to *her?*

Nothing about this made sense. Whatever amount of curiosity she'd had back in the mine to learn more about this stone was gone. The object felt hungry now, desperate, almost gluttonous in its desire for her. Thinking about holding it again made her stomach turn.

"Okay. Let's do it," Lees said finally. Meshi nodded eagerly and opened the box. Lees reached into her pouch, hesitating before touching the stone again, preparing to grab and drop it in as fast as possible.

"Wait!" Ike called out with a groan.

Meshi butted in, "Ike, it's fine. I think she can handle touching the stone long enough to contain it in here."

"Meshi, quit talking down to her." Ike barked. This is the first time he'd raised his voice. Lees held back a smirk at Meshi's shocked look. This must not be a common occurrence.

"It's Lees, right?" Ike continued. "I know you don't know me, but I need you to hear me out." The man sounded almost sad, not in a fighting-through-the-pain way, but like he was genuinely grieving something.

"That damn stone doesn't call to *people*," He said.

"Ike-" Meshi warned forcefully. Ike crawled out of bed and began to dress himself, grimacing whenever he shifted. Meshi stepped forward to block her view of Ike. He shook the box and urged, "Lees, just put the stone in here."

Lees paused. Her resolve to throw the stone away a moment ago was cracking. There *was* something he wasn't telling her. She tightened her grip on the pouch.

Ike gently put his hand on Meshi's shoulder and pushed him aside. "Meshi, you need to hold on. The girl has control of the object. She's in this now whether she likes it or not, and you have to accept that." Now that he was standing next to her, Lees could appreciate just how big Ike was. He stood at least a foot taller than her and was nearly twice as wide.

Meshi and Ike stared at each other for what felt like an eternity. Lees wasn't sure if she felt tension or agreement. *Was she in danger?*

But despite Ike's intimidating size, she strangely felt like he was a bigger threat to Meshi than her.

"It calls to a *person*," Ike finished his thought. "Singular. One. But you knew that already, right Meshi?"

Meshi's face twitched. He snapped the box closed and shoved it angrily back into his bag, that trademark sneer back on his face. With his back still to them, Meshi gripped the arms of the chair until his knuckles were white and laughed bitterly.

"Ike, you sentimental fool. You idiot. You have no survival instincts, you know that? None."

The skin on Lees' arms and the back of her neck prickled. Meshi's voice had taken on that cold tone from before. She held her breath and looked at Ike, who looked just as shocked and confused.

"I was this close," Meshi hissed.

Lees' blood ran cold. "You didn't see anything in that cave, did you?" She whispered.

"He wanted to. I'm sure of that. It's all he's ever wanted," Ike said. "You have to let it go, Meshi. There's nothing you can do now. You're a good kid, and an up-and-coming shaper. You have plenty without the object."

"You don't know what you're talking about!" Meshi shouted, slamming the chair against the ground.

"So you are a shaper," Lees muttered.

"Meshi, hang on," Ike tried to console him by reaching his hand out to touch his shoulder again.

Meshi whipped around and swatted Ike's hand away. Meshi's other hand was deep inside his duffel bag. "Get away from me!" he shouted. "You're not in charge!"

Lees caught a flash of red brass, then her eyes focused on the sharpened point directly in front of her face. Meshi had drawn a stake on them. Lees had never seen one in person, but knew enough to know these weapons were only good for one thing. Killing. It would only take a thought, barely a breath, for the sharpened rod of Hyper to erupt from the small yellow stone at its center, impaling anything in its path.

"Dammit Meshi, where did you get a thing like that?" Ike shouted.

"You lied about everything," Lees accused.

"Oh, grow up!" Meshi growled. He jabbed the stake at her. Lees gasped, but before she could move, Ike had swung his arm out to protect her.

"Move." The single word held an immense weight when Meshi spoke. Ike didn't flinch.

"Meshi, think this through. How far are you willing to go to get this thing? Is it really that important?"

"Yes! You would know that if you paid attention to anything. There is *nothing* that will get in my way of taking the Hyper Object. I would do anything," Meshi's eyes darted to the bandaged stab wound on Ike's side.

"It was you," Ike laughed hollowly. He shook his head. "Thought my mind was playing tricks on me from the pain. But it was you, wasn't it? You were the one who stabbed me in the restaurant."

The two glared at each other. Lees could practically see the tension in the room. She silently watched them face each other down, like two beasts ready to strike at any moment.

No, that wasn't quite right. There was pain in Ike's eyes, that sadness from before, whereas only rage filled Meshi's.

"Well, you caught me," Meshi said, smiling wryly and giving him an exaggerated shrug. "I figured it would make us out to be the victims and get the chippers to send me off to the mines," He nodded his head toward Lees and rolled his eyes, "Since that's basically the only thing they do or think about in this backwards town."

"Who are you?" Lees said. "Really, who are you and what do you want?"

Ike ushered Lees further behind him as Meshi looked at

her with an obnoxiously condescending face. He now stood directly in front of the only door out of the room.

"I want the Hyper Object," Meshi said slowly, enunciating every syllable as if she were a child. "Have you not been listening, or are you just as dense as him?" Meshi stepped forward again, pushing Lees and Ike further back into the room.

"See, this is how it works. He serves me. So I'm in charge of this whole situation," Meshi jabbed the stake towards them again, as if punctuating his sentence with it. "I needed to go down the mineshaft to find it, but you were in my way. I needed to break the sphere to get it, but again, you were in my way. And then, all I needed to do was touch it. Simple. But you. Were. In. My. Way!" Meshi snarled. Ike kept his arm out in front of Lees but remained still.

"You could have given it to me, put it in the box, and we could've all gone our separate ways. You back to your sad little life, and me out of this pathetic shithole. But no. You had to try and think," Meshi continued, his voice spiraling as he spoke. "And then *you,*" he pointed the stake at Ike, "had to defend this *nobody*. Your whole little altruistic act is supposed to benefit me, that's the whole reason I picked you. I'll never understand you, Ike, and now..." Meshi held up his free hand and gestured wildly.

"Seriously? This whole I'm-a-scared-new-mite-in-town act was just because you're looking to make a name for yourself back at the Oppri? Are you kidding?" Lees blurted.

Meshi grinned widely.

"You are a sad creep," Lees said, forgetting about the deadly weapon aimed at her chest. Meshi's mouth dropped in mock offense.

"You think I care what some..." He paused, mouth twisting as he tried to find an insult. "Some-some nothing thinks? You're a worthless mite. A literal piece of trash that nobody cares about. And you still dare to *stand in my way*," Meshi raised the stake to point it threateningly. "I'm done playing around. Hand over the Hyper Object or I put this rod between your eyes and move on with my day."

"Meshi, you don't have to do this. You can still walk away," Ike pleaded.

"No, Ike, I can't. Of course you don't understand, no one understands!" Meshi shouted. His face was contorted in a mixture of fury and disbelief. Lees stared at him as if looking at a stranger. Even his stance seemed different than before, shoulders hunched and knees bent, as if this anger had physically altered him.

"There are other ways to get what you want without killing an innocent woman," Ike argued.

Meshi's focus tightened on Lees. He flashed the brass stake again, and its stone shimmered as he gripped it to steady his aim.

Slowly, painfully slowly, Lees shifted her hand to rest on her hip. One finger slid under the flap of the pouch, then pressed against the snap.

It didn't matter. Meshi caught the motion, and Lees

watched as his eyes followed her hand to the pocket with the Hyper Object. Ike moved quicker than someone with his injury should be able to and closed the distance between her and Meshi. In a single motion, his left hand locked onto Meshi's wrist and thrust the stake upward. With his free hand, Ike snatched the heavy flowerpot from the bedside table and crashed it down on the crown of Meshi's head. Water, clay, and flowers exploded outward as Meshi collapsed, howling in pain.

"Go!" Ike shouted at Lees.

Meshi threw up his arms to pull Ike down. Lees jumped over Meshi to the bed, then launched herself out the door. Her head throbbed with each footfall as she stumbled out onto the clinic's front steps. She spun around, hoping to find the doctor or anyone who could help, but the area was empty.

A *crash,* followed by another, then a third, rang out from inside the doctor's office. Lees backed away. She wanted to help. Really, she did. Her brain screamed to race back in and stop Meshi, save the injured man, end the madness, but her feet kept moving, taking her further and further from the danger.

Am I that much of a coward? She thought. Am I running to protect myself, or... this stone?

Is this the stone's doing?

Lees struggled to stop and stumbled. Her foot caught on an uneven divot in the ground. Sharp pain shot up her leg as her ankle twisted the wrong way, and she fell to the ground hard.

She grabbed her ankle and sucked in a few painful breaths. The office was quiet now, but when she looked up at it, the building was completely dark.

Had it always been dark? Would Dr. Hayes have shut it down with us still inside? Lees wondered. She strained her ears, hoping to hear the dense footsteps of Gripes prowling around the grounds.

With a bang, the front door swung open. Lees whimpered and scooted back. Meshi stepped out and crossed the threshold. He brushed dirt off his shoulder and calmly walked into the flat yellow light of the town. The stake was nowhere to be seen. Neither was Ike.

No way was she going to let him catch her on the ground. Lees pulled herself up and gingerly put weight on her rolled ankle. *Sure could use the doctor right about now.*

Meshi looked at her in surprise. He froze at the top of the stairs and regarded her for a moment before cocking his head in confusion. The impostor mite looked left, then right, as if checking to see if anybody was around.

"Well, you didn't get very far," He said matter-of-factly. A wide grin spread across his face as he leered down at her.

CHAPTER 8

The Stone's Power

There was no chance her twisted ankle would hold up if she tried to run. Lees gently shifted her weight to the good ankle and tried to think around the pain.

"Where's Ike?" Lees growled.

"Oh, he needed to lie down for a bit," Meshi replied with a shrug. He started walking down the stairs toward her, his movement unhurried. "You know this could all be over if you would just give me the stone. You didn't even want it an hour ago."

Every word made Lees' blood boil. Anger surged through her body, circulating with each heartbeat. She watched him saunter forward, his hair turning almost green in the pale Rapidite light, and it was as if she could finally see him, the real Meshi. Beneath the grime from their excursion and the ill-fitting coveralls was a truly rotten, single-minded outsider with an utter lack of empathy. He used her, deceived her, and she *protected him*. She put herself in harm's way for *him*.

Without a word – *what was even the point in arguing with him anymore?* – she unsnapped the pouch on her hip. Brilliant red light spilled out from its confines.

This stopped Meshi. He eyed the pouch on her hungrily, stopping short of licking his lips as he stared. Bile rose in the back of Lees' throat. But she didn't blink.

"I'll use it."

"You're not a shaper," He smirked, but kept his eyes glued to the pouch. As if looking away would cause it to disappear.

Lees tried to swallow, but her throat was so dry she almost choked before responding.

"I've got to be something— it talked to *me*, remember? I guess you wouldn't know. You've never been called." What was meant to be an insult was undercut by the cracking in her voice.

Meshi's face scrunched into a sharp scowl. His gaze snapped back at her and he started moving again.

"Stop there. Leave my town or—"

"Or what?" Meshi taunted. His lip curled into a sneer. *Does this guy only have the one look?*

"Or I'll fight back," Lees said.

"A rematch? And I don't have to pretend to be fighting against my will?" Meshi tucked his chin, and a cruel smile crept across his face. His eyes widened in excitement. He hopped down the final step and closed the distance in two long strides. "All right then."

He swung, putting his full weight into the punch. Lees stumbled back on her hurt ankle gracelessly, but it did the trick. His right arm blew past her face, barely missing her. Meshi was already lashing out with his other arm. The second blow landed squarely in her gut and knocked the air out of her lungs. In the same motion, Lees doubled over in pain and slapped a hand on the back of his neck, then yanked hard.

Meshi slammed to the ground but sprang to his feet immediately. Lees winced at the flash of pain from her hurt ankle, and he took advantage of the moment. He tackled Lees and aimed a knee at the twisted ankle. Lees yelped and the duo fell hard, limbs tangling and their wriggling bodies kicking up dust.

A singular point of red light bounced around them. The Hyper Object had jostled free of the pouch and landed a few feet away. Flashes of excited light caught their attention, and there was a moment of awkward pushing and kicking as they both tried to reach it.

Lees dug her shoulder into the ground and pushed against Meshi with her back enough to reach the stone. The asshole wriggled one arm free and grabbed her wrist. He slammed her arm against the ground hard once, twice, before gaining enough momentum to flip her over.

Meshi rolled to his feet. Lees grabbed his ankle and dug

her thumb into his Achilles tendon, pressing hard enough for her nail to break skin. He buckled and fell to his knees. Ignoring the searing pain shooting up her shin, Lees grabbed Meshi's shoulders to pull herself up and over, fighting to untangle herself from him. He kicked backward, catching her in the thigh. She lost balance, slamming into him with her full weight. Meshi crumpled beneath her. Lees dug her knee into his back, then finally pulled herself back up and away from him.

Breathing hard now, blood pounding in her ears, Lees calculated she had about three seconds to escape with the stone before he got up. She lurched forward to grab it, but just like down in the mine, her math was wrong.

Meshi loomed behind her, threw his arm around her throat, and squeezed.

All thoughts ceased, all focus vanished. She gasped for breath that would not come. Her lungs seized with the lack of airflow, the lack of breath, the beginning stages of suffocation.

He squeezed tighter and tighter. Lees clawed at his arm, barely hearing the wet choking sounds she was making. Pinpoints of darkness swarmed at the edges of her vision. Her chest was on fire. Her chest was collapsing.

The tighter he squeezed, the more desperate her flailing. Nails snagged shirt and skin, leaving bloody trails down his arm, but Meshi persisted. Lees thrust her head back, but he jerked his away in time. To her right. Her elbow swung back and connected with his nose almost before she could think to do it. Bone crunched sickeningly, and Meshi fell away with a strangled scream.

Air rushed back into her lungs. Lees gasped as she gently touched the swollen skin on her neck, tried to massage away the assault.

Red light fluttered in the periphery of her vision. The stone began bouncing slightly, almost vibrating, when she looked directly at it.

"I'b going to bucking kill you," Meshi's voice was muffled as he gargled out the threat. Blood poured out beneath the hand clamped around his broken nose, then flowed freely down his lips and throat when he removed it. He bared his teeth, stained with his own blood.

Lees scrambled backward from the deranged sight of him until she reached the stone. She slammed her palm down to grab it and held it to her chest. Meshi moved toward her with a murderous look, reaching into his pocket for who knows what.

Every breath felt like inhaling razor blades. Her lungs protested with each breath sucked through her bruised throat. She couldn't get her breathing under control, every inhale too shallow and every exhale too painful. Lees couldn't fight him off, this bloodied stranger fueled by an animalistic rage. She curled into the fetal position, squeezing her eyes closed with the stone tight in her fist.

"Please help me," She whispered, her voice low and hoarse.

With a blinding pulse of red light, the Hyper Object consumed Lees. A thick protective cocoon wrapped around her before Meshi could reach her.

Meshi screamed so shrilly that it sounded like his throat split in two. His fists came down on the barrier, blow after blow, but the sound was muted and getting quieter. The shooting pain in her leg and soreness in her chest and burning in her throat eased until all sensation melted away. Until she could feel and hear nothing through the barrier.

She remained in this position, soaking in the silence. Her breathing slowed and steadied. Eventually, Lees became aware of one thing outside of herself. The Hyper Object moved in her hand, like a bramble chick fluttering, curling, and rolling over itself.

Nothing existed beyond the barrier as far as Lees was concerned. She opened her eyes to total darkness.

No, not quite true, she thought. Small red particles shimmered in the air all around. She sat up in a rush and opened her hands— but the stone was gone.

A yawning, creaking sound shattered the silence from somewhere behind her. Lees turned with a start.

The enormous crystal hand flinched with her sudden movement. It retracted into the darkness, its fingers shifting slightly at the edge of visibility. There was something noticeably different in the way it moved now.

"Hello again," Lees croaked. She was surprised to find her heart was beating normally. She wasn't scared.

Should she be scared...?

No response came. She finally stood up, taking care to move slowly so as not to spook the hand, and realized happily that her ankle supported her weight just fine. Keeping one eye on the crystal hand hovering in front of her, she looked around. No question about it. She was back in the void.

"This is crazy, but... are you the stone?" Lees asked. She took a tentative step forward. The hand didn't move.

"Where did you take me?" Lees asked, sharper than intended. "I mean, thank you. You saved me from him. I really think he would have killed me."

It was Lees' turn to flinch as the pain and adrenaline of the fight flashed before her. Meshi's hands wrapping around her throat, the bruises she undoubtedly had that matched each of his squeezing, relentless fingers. The nausea-inducing smack on the back of her skull as she hammered it against his face. *His face.*

Meshi's face appeared before her. It was larger than life, refracting off the different facets of this void dome. His mouth opened wide, exposing teeth as big as her head, and he laughed.

"You can't control it," He jeered.

"You'll fail. You're nothing. And it will consume you like you're nothing."

His voice was impossibly loud in her head now, like

distorted feedback at earsplitting volume. She clamped her hands over her ears and lost balance, dropping to her knees in pain as his projected face spun around her. He laughed and laughed as each twinge of pain flickered across her body – throat, chest, knee, ankle, head.

Meshi's fists slammed down on the dome, now a giant with bone-crushing hands.

"Stop! If this is you, please, stop this!" Lees whined.

The minuscule red particles in the air spun in a flurry before her. It swarmed, obliterating the laughing face that donned a look of horror before it disappeared. Lees covered her eyes as the collection whipped around her, but then she heard another voice.

"Lees, are you okay!?"

She wrenched her eyes open. Teeg was kneeling in front of her in his patched work apron, his thick eyebrows knitted with concern as he traced the cuts and bruises covering her. He reached out to her.

Lees opened her mouth, but what was there to say? He found her, twice in one day, came to rescue her when she needed him most. Her breath hitched, and relief flooded her veins. She leaped forward to embrace him, to let him carry her out of here, take her home–

And fell right through him to the cold, flat floor of the void.

Tears welled up from frustration and disappointment in equal measure, and she let them fall freely down her cheeks. The vision of Teeg remained, kneeling away from her, one enormous hand still outstretched. Then he disappeared in a swirl of red sand.

"Are you trying to hurt me? Was M—was *he* right?" She whispered.

A wave of regret washed over her, but the emotion felt distant.

Lees leaned back on one elbow and wiped the tears from her face. She sniffled, then nodded.

"Alright. You've made your point. You can be in control," She said, a moment before it occurred to her that this might be unwise. What does that actually mean?

The red swarm bobbed in the air once, twice, then spread back out around her.

She cleared her throat and took a deep breath. Turning to the hand still hovering motionless at the edge of the void, she said matter-of-factly, "Take me home."

The void swelled to life, and a flurry of colors rushed past Lees. The sand reformed into a soft wooden floor that clattered outwards, board by board. Next, a series of arching windows bent over her head, and she looked through them onto her old neighborhood in the Quarters!?

A scuffed but clean wooden table stretched out before her. Dozens of plants in pots of every size lined the room. Odd bulbous mushrooms, vines with razor-sharp teeth, and even a miniature wortwood tree in an oversized pot in the corner near a window.

Lees' mouth was suddenly dry. She knew this room. She

had it memorized, down to the uneven square nails in the floorboards near the entryway. Her heart fluttered as she looked around.

There she was. Perched on a three-legged stool with a checkered cover on the seat. Legs crossed beneath her. Wavy shoulder-length hair cut unevenly at the ends, frizzy and curling around her ears, just like Lees'. Shoulders rounded from years spent hunched over a small workbench, like she was right now, expertly shaping something. Long, delicate fingers working the Hyper methodically.

Her heart swelled, instantly choking her up. Lees swallowed hard, blinking back a fresh wave of tears.

"Mom?" She said softly, not wanting to startle her. Her mother didn't respond or give any indication that she knew Lees was there.

Of course she didn't. She wasn't real. This wasn't real.

"Why are you showing me this!?" Lees shouted. Technically, the Hyper Object was all around her, so Lees tilted her head back and issued the question at her childhood ceiling for all the good it did. "Are you just toying with me? You need to let me go, I need to get out of here."

The room began to break apart into those tiny red particles, just like Teeg had. Right before it vanished entirely, her mom turned to look over her shoulder. Lees hurried forward to reach her before it was too late, but the woman dissipated before she could reach her. Lees stood in the dark void again, one arm outstretched, cold waves of disappointment crashing against her.

Alone. Again. Is this what the Hyper Object did? Taunt her with the people she loved most? Her mother, Teeg, then down in the cave, Jez —

The sand began to spin wildly as if suddenly excited. Out of the chaos, the saloon owner appeared before her. Jez leaned against the bar and flipped her long hair over her shoulder, simultaneously pouring a beer and laughing at something someone said. She slid the beer across the counter to the waiting patron and winked. Lees knew this wasn't real, knew this was just the Hyper Object showing her what she wanted, but she couldn't help herself. She stayed in the vision, spending a few precious moments admiring the way Jez effortlessly moved behind the bar, keeping a watchful eye on everyone in the Eye of Mite.

"She's so amazing," Lees said softly without thinking.

Jez turned to her with a look of confusion. No, not confusion. Disgust. Jez's lip curled as she looked her up and down. Lees' heart sank.

Why is this stone tormenting me?

White-hot pain exploded across her jaw. The force of it knocked her off balance. Before Lees hit the ground, the vision of Jez vanished in a swirl of sand.

The bitter taste of iron flooded her mouth, filling the space she would have needed to cry out. She didn't have time to process what was happening before being bombarded by a series of visions. Her parents' faces filled with shame when they finally realized that her skill was never going to manifest. Her mother comforting her, but the words didn't match the disappointment in her eyes. Her father slamming his hands on the kitchen counter, denting the draining board and breaking her mother's favorite mug. Memories seared into the folds of her brain, memories she pushed into the corner of her mind and left to fester.

Lees wanted to say something, anything, but choked on the blood in her mouth. She could only let out a guttural moan when the wet thump of a sharp blow caved in her stomach. Instant nausea seized her guts, sending her tumbling over herself.

"Having a little trouble discerning what's real?" Meshi's voice pierced the darkness, distorted and echoing. A tendon running across her elbow sizzled, sending prickling shocks down to her fingers. Something dug into the delicate skin of her inner wrist.

Where is he? Is he in here with me? Lees whipped her head around, but the infinite void pressed in on her.

Another vision, this one of her, a twisted funhouse version of herself on the day she was ripped away from her home. Manhandled onto the train, then pushed out of the car onto the platform at Last Light. The chippers standing shoulder-to-shoulder in the entryway, as if ready to block any attempt to reboard.

Lees' stomach somersaulted at the sensation of being

shoved. She watched herself stumble, then fell forward herself. And again. And again. Rewinding and replaying, her own private viewing.

"Get up!" She gurgled, both to herself and the version of her at the station. Her hands and knees stung with friction burns from falling to the ground over and over.

There was something hard in her left hand. She was surprised to see that her fist was clenched hard, white-knuckling without her consent or direction.

Meshi surged before her, and without thinking, Lees swung her fist at him. The boy dispersed, then reformed at her side. The sand mirage of Meshi swept his leg at her – through her – and a corresponding blow, a real one, landed right above her kidney.

Then he rematerialized and did it again. Countless times. He grabbed her throat again, he twisted her arm back until it popped, he knelt to help her up, he held her down and poured liquid poison into her bruised mouth. Heat seared the back of her exposed neck. She choked out a yelp in protest as a brutal weight crushed her fingers.

Lees couldn't think, couldn't move, was powerless to react through the blinding agony. There was no way to tell what was real besides the pain threatening her sanity.

"You shouldn't have grabbed the stone, you worthless mite," Meshi's words echoed through her mind. Lees looked up through swollen eyes at his cold, blank expression.

Worthless. Mite.

CHAPTER 9
Warped Visions

A tiny, angry voice in the back of Lees' mind began to scream, to fight, to buck against the assault. It grew louder and angrier until it consumed her, so aggressive that it swept the pain to the side. Lees took a deep breath and bellowed, "GET AWAY FROM ME!" At the same time, she extended her arm to push the threat away.

The Hyper Object bubbled and burst in her clenched fist, melting into her hand and squeezing through the cracks in her fingers like dough.

Red-sand-mirage Meshi tried to dodge, but the Hyper Object was much too fast for that. Waterlike tendrils wrapped around Lees' hand, covering her fist in a dense crystal before erupting outward.

With all the strength she could muster, Lees swung the crystal fist at him once again. A pulse of blood-red light erupted as a towering pillar of pure Hyper connected with the boy.

Her world exploded. An ear-splitting explosion rocked her. The force of it was so great that it shattered the dark void surrounding her.

Inky blackness slunk away. Pale yellow light filtered in. Slowly, the clinic and wraparound porch, then the buildings beyond its railing, came into view. She was standing in Last Light, her feet planted firmly on the real ground. With a start, she held up her arm and stared at the stone extending from it.

Meshi groaned pitifully, then fell silent. Lees almost didn't see him, he'd been knocked so far away. His body had hit the ground with such force Lees could see the long trail he'd made in the dirt. One leg stuck out at an unnatural position. His shredded shirt revealed a ragged puncture wound in his side. She could barely make out his features through the dirt and blood.

Despite the gore, Lees watched him warily, waiting for the next move. His next trick. She dropped her arm to hand limply at her side. The stone tendrils dripped and pooled on the ground, but she kept her eyes on Meshi. It was nauseating to look at him, every moment her eyes trailing along another horrible injury, but she forced herself to stay vigilant.

But it didn't come. The boy was still breathing, but barely.

Lees dropped to the ground from the weight of the Hyper,

exhausted. Blood dripped out of her palm and flowed across the stone's sharp points. Tiny beads of it slipped between the stone's folding layers as it shifted in on itself.

It didn't hurt, but it felt odd.

Lees tried to pull her hand free, but the Hyper wouldn't budge.

"Thanks for the help. Really. But you can let me go now," She groaned. It didn't respond. She placed her foot on top of the pillar and pulled hard to free herself.

Barbs of Hyper stabbed her palm and forearm. Dozens of points slid into her all at once with little effort, the needling pain spreading up her arm like venom. Lees frantically clawed at the Hyper, panic rising in her chest.

"Hey, stop! Stop it!" She shouted.

Visions chattered along the edges of her vision. Crystal enveloping her battered body entirely, her eyes still visible but now glowing red, and Meshi cowering before her.

Lees shook her head and jumped to her feet, then grabbed her elbow to drag the heavy stone back.

"Release me!" She commanded, but the stone crept further up her arm. Her mind flashed with images again. Meshi choking her out, a crystalline blade piercing her stomach, Teeg's workshop on fire.

"That's not going to happen!" Lees argued, half-blinded by the onslaught of fearful visions. The stone didn't budge.

New sounds of voices and hurried footsteps shook her from her thoughts. Dozens of miners stood on the nearby terrace, staring at the clinic's patio where she stood. Fear was etched on their faces as they looked at her, like they were staring at a monster.

Lees froze, her breathing suddenly staggered and heavy. A large knot coiled itself inside her chest, a snake lying in wait since she'd arrived in this town. The threat of isolation looming, tauntingly closing in.

Someone was pushing their way through the crowd.

"Lees! Hey, Lees!" Teeg shouted. He jostled a few people and growled, "Move!" before breaking through to the front of the group.

For a moment, Lees wondered if any of this was real. She'd been shown Teeg twice before now, and here he stood again, the man who had taken her in and protected her for two years, looking at her with a horrified expression. Mouth agape, eyes wide.

Was this another trick?

Images filled her mind. This was real, the stone seemed to assure her. But Teeg hated her. He would kick her out. He saw her as a monster. It was all there, laid out neatly, a chronological depiction of her exile from this moment forward.

Lees' heart sank. The stone tightened its grip to consume her upper arm.

She couldn't bear to see the look on Teeg's face any longer. She looked back at Meshi's mangled body instead, a reminder of the savagery she'd just committed. Her eyes darted back and forth, all around the area, looking for an escape. In her frantic search, she spied a path through the nearby alleyway.

There was nothing else to do. Her body sprang to life as if on autopilot. Tears streamed down her face, but she could barely feel them. She ran clumsily into the dark passage, dragging the heavy Hyper arm along the ground as she went. With a small amount of pride, Lees managed to clear a solid distance despite its weight and her fatigue. She wanted to look back, but didn't have the luxury. She couldn't. Seeing Teeg's face would be too much to handle.

She hobbled over to the alley wall and slumped down.

The brick wall was cold on Lees' back. Even with her eyes squeezed shut, the visions didn't cease. Her head was filled with sand, and her mind swirled with thought after thought, each one more invasive than the last. They piled on top of one another, cluttering into a jumbled mess of ideas. Like the Hyper Object itself was trying to work something out, to show her something.

Stop, she pleaded. She was losing control.

Snippets of words, faces, smells, feelings. Were these her memories, or the Hyper Object's?

A chipper blowing his whistle, followed by the red flashing train crossing sign. Being pressed against a boulder careening down a hill, screaming in pain as her arms buckled under its weight.

No, stop. Please. Release me.

Couplings breaking. The BurgerMaker 5000 breaking apart into a thousand pieces. Her father turning to go back to bed as she was yanked through her home by the chipper escorts. Steam pouring from the morning train as it squealed to a stop at a littered station.

Her arm throbbed as the Hyper wrapped itself tighter, encasing her little by little. She leaned to the side but over-corrected and tipped over into an overflowing garbage bag. It was the most comfortable and serene embrace from trash she'd ever received.

Lees opened her eyes a crack and saw the blurry shape of two people approaching. They were definitely coming toward her.

"Don't. Leave," She mouthed. The shadows descended upon her, suddenly right next to her.

Get away. Get off me!

Lees watched herself ripping at the Hyper, shredding her fingers on its sharp edges. Something overtook her, and she screamed in retaliation. Spikes of Hyper burst out in all directions. Wood splintered, stone crumbled, and one of the figures yelped in pain. Exhaustion tore at her, and Lees slumped back.

"Damnit! Don't move," A man's voice said.

"Not like I have a choice," A woman responded with an edge of sarcasm. Those dulcet tones were familiar.

A vision of Jez appeared to Lees, wearing a low-cut shirt and shiny red shoes. She was perched on top of a large slice of citrus fruit, floating in space with her long hair blowing in the wind.

"But *you* do!" Jez's voice bellowed out, her enthusiastic tone mimicking an infomercial spokesperson. "We know that you can choose any old brew from the Oppri, so we wanted to thank you for drinking VineTek Craft Pilsner, now with lime!" From atop the fruit, she cracked open a can of beer and giggled as it sprayed across her neck and collarbone.

"Heh heh, what are you doing on that fruit, Jez?" Lees muttered.

"Hun, I need you to come back now," The image of the fruit-mounted Jez said to Lees.

You can hear me? Lees responded in her mind.

"Lees, please wake up," Fruit-Jez wound an arm around Lees to help her sit up. The foaming beer bubbles faded away to a crimson black static.

"I'ss got m'good, Jez," Lees' tongue felt heavy. Pushing the words out was taking too much effort. This couldn't be real, but she chose to believe the lie and sink into Jez's warm embrace. It was the least the stone could do for her.

"I know, but you're stronger than that," Fruit-Jez said. She smiled as she did, and continued to smile even as one of her front teeth fell out of her mouth and her eyes went white.

"Ew, nooo, I'on't like that part," Lees muttered. "Ge' back on the fruit."

"What is she saying?" A low voice rumbled.

"Lees, I need you to focus. Tell me what's on your arm,"

despite having no teeth left in her mouth, Jez continued to speak without issue.

"It's this sssstupid rock!" Lees shouted indignantly.

The woman's voice screamed again, louder than before. Lees' vision swam with an image of a red stone tendril burrowing deeper into someone's leg. "Who'sat? Why're you hurtin' them?"

"Focus," Jez groaned. Bright lights erupted as Lees felt a sharp slap on her cheek. She looked up in wonderment at Jez, whose head had morphed into a lifelike statue of Hyper. This new form spoke with the jarring sounds of metal scraping on metal. "Tell me about this rock."

"I fought the rich boy." A bell rang somewhere. It vibrated inside Lees' body and made the bones rattle in her head.

"That kid from the bar?" The bell came again.

"I'n't mean to... He just wouldn't stop," Lees said, straining to keep her thoughts straight. Meshi stood behind metal-Jez, pointing the stake at her menacingly. She blinked, and the mess of his body lay crumpled in the alley. Another blink, and his body rose up like a ghoul to stalk away into the night.

The bell rang in rapid succession. Clang, clang, clang. She tried to move. She needed to get up!

"Wait, wait, wait. We have'ta hurry. He's going to hurt more people," She could hear the woman in front of her panting and groaning now. "Is someone hurting that woman!?"

"Woodro, stop! You won't be able to cut through it," The

woman growled. It sounded fractal and distant. "Go find the boy."

There was a long silence now. Lees could only see darkness.

Then Jez's voice broke through. "Lees, you got that stone in your hand now?" She asked. Her voice sounded normal again. Lees thought she nodded, but she might have just slumped forward. Did Jez think that was cool? "Okay, great. Can you drop it? Just let go."

Her brain erupted in a frenzy. Spikes of Hyper shot out from the void towards her. She scrambled back on her raw and bloodied hands and knees. Meshi's voice called out from the darkness, mocking her. Stalking closer. *I'm coming to kill you,* he sang. She saw the train, cutlass knights pouring out its open doors by the hundreds. Their silver armor and masked faces shimmered under the pale yellow light as they infiltrated Last Light. Her home.

Lees' breath quickened, her chest rising and falling in rapid succession, careening toward hyperventilating. A river of snot flowed from her nose to her lips. Her eyes welled up with hot tears as she sobbed out, "I can't. I can't! They'll kill everyone, I can't let them."

"Whoa, hey, slow down. Breathe. It's all right," Jez said. She placed her hands on Lees' shoulders and gently rubbed them. Her voice had an edge, like she was gritting her teeth. "We ain't gonna take that rock from you. I don't want it. All I need you to do is open your hand and let it drop."

"Just... drop?"

"That's right. Just drop it. Nobody will take it," Jez assured her.

Lees stared with singular focus at her hand encased in the crystal. She tried to will it to open. Countless spikes of the Hyper Object were embedded deep in her fingers and palm, and though it curiously hadn't hurt before, opening each finger to pull them out was shockingly painful. Taking a deep breath in through her nose, Lees blocked out the pain to open one finger at a time. She rotated her hand slowly downward, turning the weight of the crystal with it. From this angle, the Hyper Object resembled a stubborn bramble clinging to her palm.

"That's it, good girl. Just keep-" Jez cut herself off with a groan of pain.

"What's wrong? Are you hurt?" Lees asked. An image more like a command shot to the front of her mind – *clamp your hand shut. There's danger here. Jez is hurt.*

"No, no! Lees, listen to me," Jez's voice was so much closer to her now. Almost whispering in her ear. "Nothing is wrong. I won't let anything happen to you."

No blows came. No bursts of pain. No crushed fingers or broken bones. Just Jez's hands still rubbing soothing circles down her back.

I trust you, Lees thought. The stone clattered to the ground.

Lees' mind went blank. For a blissful moment, she felt

nothing but Jez's body against hers. Then a deafening ringing filled her ears, and the world suddenly seemed too bright.

Lees squinted at the light as her eyes came to focus and she sat up.

"Oh, wow, my head is pounding, I'm exhausted," Lees looked down at her arm expecting to see Hyper encasing it, but only saw the small stone sitting on the dark cobble in front of her.

"First time hits ya hard, doesn't it?" Jez said. Her words rattled around Lees' head, but didn't make sense.

Lees stood up too quickly and had to lean against the wall until the fit of dizziness subsided. She looked down to catch Jez wrapping her leg with her torn shirt sleeve.

"Are you hurt? What happened?" Lees moved to help her, but Jez waved her off and reached out for a hand up.

"I'll be fine. Just a nick," Jez stood up with a wince.

"That's more than a nick—you've been stabbed in the thigh!" Lees' face dropped with the realization. "It was me. I hurt you. You were the woman yelling in my vision."

"You didn't mean to. Now, put your glove on and pocket that damn rock. We need to get somewhere safe," Jez snapped. She walked with a limp, and Lees fought the urge to help her, knowing she'd be reprimanded. She didn't like it, but she did what she was told.

Vol. 1 Bonus Chapter

Dark Dealings

Before arriving in Last Light, Meshi and Ike had spent weeks on the road searching for clues. By the time they arrived in Ulteck City the duo was running out of patience and connections. That is, until an unexpected revelation led them to one of the deepest mining towns in the world.

Read this bonus chapter for free at:

hyperobject.ink/dark-dealings

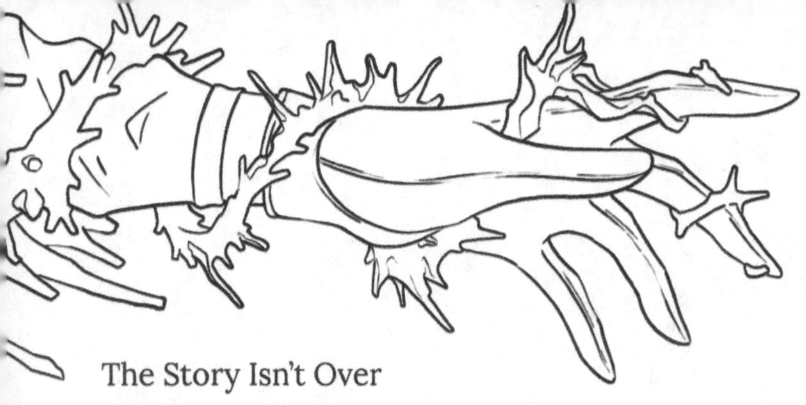

Your next adventure in the Keeperverse is coming soon.

If you're enjoying Hyper Object, here is a sneak preview from our upcoming book Keeper.

Hazel's world is disappearing. The phenomenon eliminating Traxia piece by piece is accelerating, and the Keepers are powerless to stop it. Frustrated by the Council's inaction,

Hazel disobeys orders to investigate herself – and ends up face-to-face with an enemy that hasn't been seen in decades. With the help of her reluctant companions, Hazel must find a way to recover her powers and save two worlds from destruction.

The Witch Hazel

High up in the mountains, the late morning sun illuminated a region that was perfectly still, save for one lone figure winding its way through the trees.

Hazel wasn't technically supposed to be out here alone. Standard expedition protocol along the northern mountain region called for Keepers to be accompanied by a minimum of two Traxian soldiers. Mt. Tuocs' peak rose high above the cloudline, and the sharp drop-offs and thin air created tricky situations for the careless.

Since this wasn't an official mission, she reasoned that this wasn't exactly breaking protocol. That hadn't stopped her from taking precautions by waking up before first bells and taking the longer, more cumbersome route here.

The fresh snow on the mountainside sparkled in the light of the rising sun, and Hazel delighted in crunching through the untouched snow blanketing the little forested valley between peaks. She moved briskly to stave off the cold. Every breath billowed out in white plumes around her face, and her cheeks burned despite the thick yellow cloak pulled tightly up over her face. Not even the trees growing in dense clusters this high up could slow the icy wind whipping through the valley.

Hazel was taller than most Keepers her age if you measured up to the tips of her triangular ears. Usually this worked in her favor, but traveling through the forest meant it slowed her down. She'd been constantly ducking low-slung branches and brushing away needle-line leaves caught in her fur all morning. Despite the distractions, Hazel carefully scrutinized each tree and plant for signs of disease or distress as she walked.

"Traxia?" Hazel called, craning her neck to survey the full height of a nearby tree. She traced one finger along the counterclockwise swirls in its bark. "Those amber cankers on the *ymrots pines* here, is that a fungus? Looks like it's spreading upward and drying out the branches."

<Yes, Hazel,> the Source Traxia responded.

Hazel unconsciously swiped at the fur on her right temple, a habit she'd formed as a child when a piece of the Source's power had first entered her body. When she became a Keeper and accepted the Source, Traxia's voice had hung uncomfortably between her ears like a deep itch she couldn't scratch. But that was years ago. She'd long since gotten used to the sensation.

"Tell me what's causing it."

Her vision clouded as the Source flashed a looping

animation in her head. Tiny cartoon-like spores traveled up through the severed roots of a tree before spreading to other trees nearby.

<Root damage appears to be the culprit. The damage created an entry point for the fungal spores and weakened the tree's defenses,> Traxia continued.

"It'll spread if we leave it. Traxia, cull the infected limbs and draw out the spores – minimize further damage to the tree when you do and seal up any wounds. Oh, and bubble the spores," Hazel commanded. She crouched and held her hands near the tree's base. The familiar sensation of the Source stretched out from her fingers as it pulled the spores from beneath the bark. Though she couldn't see it, Hazel could feel the nearly invisible particles follow a reverse path from their entry points before they swirled before her. A perfect transparent bubble appeared around the spores. Hazel tucked the bubble into the pouch slung over her shoulder.

While this tree might survive today, others would suffer a similar fate. Not just on this mountainside, where Hazel had been attempting to heal the damage for weeks, but across the region and beyond. Unless they could figure out a way to stop what was severing underground root structures and sapping away water, minerals, and life, it was only a matter of time before the entire forest died.

Hazel continued forward, noting every bent branch and wilted plant on the forest floor. Something was whining nearby – a desperate, high-pitched sound that cut through the frigid stillness. She snapped to attention and rushed forward.

At the edge of a small clearing, tangled in the roots of a twisted tree, a horned goat was bleating and struggling to free its antlers. The animal was just a few feet in length with disproportionately large horns jutting out of its forehead. It seemed as though the rest of its body had not quite caught up with the growth. One of the horns was hooked around an exposed root and held the animal nearly pinned to the ground. A cluster of berry bushes grew tantalizingly close, as if a carefully laid trap.

"Traxia, how old is this little fella? Has his venom come in yet, or can I touch him?"

<This horned mountain goat appears to be approximately one year old. At this age, its venom would likely knock you unconscious for several hours. I would suggest you avoid being gored. With the low temperatures in this area, you would likely perish before – >

"Yeah, yeah, thanks, got it," Hazel interrupted.

She slowed her approach and tried to move as calmly as possible, taking care to steer clear of the venomous points of its antlers. The horned goat's eyes widened as Hazel closed the distance and it thrashed wildly.

"Hey, hey, it's ok. Sorry little guy, looks like you're in quite a mess," She whispered gently. "Will you let me help you out?"

Hazel sat back on her heels and rested both hands flat

against the loose blue material of her pants. She stayed stock still for a moment, avoiding eye contact with the terrified creature, and looked for signs of pain or an injury. The creature stopped struggling and rolled its yellow eyes toward her, then let out a low whine. Hazel crawled forward and circled around to reach the bushes. She plucked a cluster from its depths and held it out toward the trapped creature.

The trapped goat hesitated, eyed Hazel suspiciously, then reached forward to devour the berries. Hazel seized the moment of distraction and grasped the trapped horn firmly at its base. The goat screeched and bucked again, but Hazel held on. Working as quickly as she could, Hazel pulled back the troublesome root and threaded the horn from its grasp.

"Traxia, put up a shield the moment I let go... just in case," Hazel murmured. She took a deep breath and let go, simultaneously propelling herself backward in the snow.

Now free, the horned goat thrashed once more. The vicious point of its venomous horn punctured the space where Hazel's face had just been before bouncing off what appeared to be an invisible barrier. It shook its head comically, then bleated once more before bounding off.

"You can drop the shield now," Hazel said.

<Understood. I am required to inform you that was an unnecessary risk,> Traxia stated.

"There's no way it would have freed itself. My job is to keep and protect. That's what I'm doing," Hazel scoffed.

Her knees were soaked from kneeling in the snow, and

the tips of her fingers were losing feeling. She hopped up and down and rubbed her hands together before covering her ears. The velvety tips burned as she massaged warmth back into them. She looked up toward the tops of the trees swaying high above her in the freezing wind that was cutting through the thick material of her pants. Hazel bounced around like this for a moment, calculating whether it was worth it to expend the energy to summon an insulated shell or portable fire. *On one hand, warmer is nice,* she mused to herself. *But on the other, if I miscalculate and pass out, the last thing I need is to be rescued by –*

Hazel's thoughts were interrupted by an ear-splitting ringing sound emanating from within her own head.

<You requested an alert when we were within one hour of the ceremony. This is your alert. We should start our journey back to the city now,> Traxia said.

"Jeez, that was way too loud. Anyway, we've got time, I want to finish up here," Hazel said dismissively. Not wanting to give in by asking Traxia for heat, she rubbed her arms vigorously once more, then continued on.

The slightly-illicit journey's destination was just ahead. With every step, the ambient noises of the forest around her dimmed. No forest animal chittered from the trees or scurried through the undergrowth. A twinge of tension flared in her left shoulder and a familiar pit of unease gurgled in her stomach. Two more steps, and the tree line abruptly ended. Hazel now stood in complete, unnatural silence.

What lay ahead looked like the aftermath of some otherworldly disaster. A sharp, perfect line stretched nearly a quarter mile wide from this spot and extended hundreds of feet beyond – a perfect square of emptiness, as if the patch of land had been neatly cut out by some malevolent giant. Skeletons of severed trees decorated one side of this line, each one having been cleaved in half with almost surgical precision.

It had been thirty years since the phenomenon first happened. A brilliant light stretched down from the sky to outline an acre of grassland, the shape perfectly symmetrical. Within hours, the illuminated square of land vanished, leaving behind a burnt, desolate patch of nothingness. It was incomprehensible. There was no lightning, no fire, no sinkhole, no disaster to speak of. One moment it was there, and the next... it wasn't.

Then it happened again a year later, this time cleanly severing a rushing river stretching from one coast to the other. This one caused problems for the thousands of Traxians relying on the flow of fresh water, and emergency services were dispatched to help. It took the Keepers a month to carve and redirect the river.

The Traxian people had no end of colorful, dramatic names for this phenomenon: The Blight, the Desolation, Atia's Wrath, the Burning. But perhaps to tamp down panic, the Council preferred their soldiers, Keepers, and scholars to simply use *dead zones* in their reports.

Hazel stood at the threshold of this dead zone and

prepared herself. She instructed the Source to pull a one-foot cube of undergrowth from the healthy side before stepping over the slice line, letting the cube of plantlife float in front of her.

"All right, you know the drill. Give me a full scan. Let's see if anything's changed," Hazel commanded.

The Source hummed in her head before a vision appeared in front of her eyes – a green grid stretched across the ground in front of her now with text scrolling along the bottom of her field of vision. Someone on the outside unfamiliar with Keepers would see Hazel standing stock still save for her tail, which flicked toward the right. But in Hazel's mind, Traxia was rapidly sharing updated information about the ground around her.

<*Calcium carbonate. Quartz fragments. Granite. Sand. Silicate,*> Traxia rattled off in a monotone voice. <*Nearly identical to the fourteen other analysis instances, Hazel. No organic material beyond what you introduced is detected.*>

"You're sure? Nothing? Not even nitrogen?"

<*Correct.*>

Hazel's stomach flipped. That assessment meant she knew even before approaching that the experiment was failing. Eight weeks ago, she'd begun planting a grid of 47 cubes identical to the one floating in front of her in the center of this dead zone. Once the Council had finished their assessment of the dead zone and vacated the area, she had snuck away to conduct her own tests. Whenever she could get away to visit, Hazel took cubes of healthy plant matter and planted them in the destroyed soil, taking care to meticulously water each one and measure its sun exposure. Up close now, only browning and wilting leaves stretched out weakly from the blackened dirt. With a nagging sense that all she was accomplishing was torturing and killing plants pulled from healthy soil, Hazel commanded the Source to dig out a square and bury the new cube.

A rain cloud formed above the little plot with a flick of Hazel's wrist, and she frowned as the water drizzled over the other plants in their various stages of death.

"So the fertilizer isn't working. We're not going to be able to reseed these dead zones, are we?"

What was going to happen when dead zones covered half the planet? Alumast and the other major cities were already overcrowded with displaced Traxians. Rivers had already been severed. Trade routes demolished. There was no rhyme or reason to where these swaths of wasteland appeared, which meant it was nearly impossible to predict where or when the beams of light appeared to signal the beginning of disaster. If they couldn't reseed, if they couldn't stop them from coming, how would they feed everybody? What would they do when habitats were destroyed? What —

A shrill siren sounded from just behind her forehead.

<We are within a half-hour of the ceremony. If you want to attend, you must leave now,> Traxia said.

"Gah - I need to change that alarm command. I'm almost done, then we can go," Hazel grumbled.

The rain cloud disappeared with a wave of her hand. She stared out at the withering plants and watched water droplets fall from their sagging stalks, trying not to feel hopeless. Though she'd set out before the sun rose this morning, it had taken nearly half the morning to reach this spot from the nearest teleporter. Hazel's tail twitched with impatience, a habit the Orator had scolded her for since childhood. There wasn't enough time to get everything done, especially not unsanctioned work. If she could just take a moment, just have space to think, she could figure out the next move...

"Maybe we're missing pollinators," She mused. But no living creature in the area would come close to the dead zone, even though it had been here for months. Bringing in the insects and other critters these plants relied on might help in the short-term, but what if those ended up dying, too? Hazel's chest tightened as an involuntary image of corpses littering the dead zone popped into her head – No, she couldn't risk that.

<Hazel, based on the command you issued this morning, we must leave now,> Traxia insisted loudly.

"FINE!" Hazel shouted. Her voice bounced around the empty space. "Let's fly to Alumast."

<Taking the teleporter might be faster, if you want to –>

"No, let's fly. Use the command set Flying Falcon Cloak."

Regardless of the Source's warnings or recommendations,

Keepers were the ones in control. At her command, the Source flowed through her and extended beyond her own body. Behind her, Hazel's cloak parted with a satisfying snap. Debris on the forest floor – tiny pebbles and bits of minerals – rose and flew toward her to reinforce the fabric as it hardened into sharp curved wings spreading on either side of her. The front of her cloak wrapped around over and under her arms, securing the wings to her torso. She flexed her arms, making the faux wings shift and twitch with the movement.

<Ready when you are, Hazel,> Traxia said flatly.

Hazel jumped into the air with impressive speed and used her hands to manipulate the air around and below her to launch her skyward. Within seconds, the Source-aided breeze brought her hundreds of feet above her dead zone project. Frustration clouded her mind for a moment, but flying was the best way to clear her mind. She arched her wings and shot toward the ground, pulling up just above the snow-capped treeline. She looped once, twice, then jetted off toward the horizon in the direction of the city.

Acknowledgements

We want to thank all of our friends and family for their support and encouragement on this project. You've helped push us to create something beautiful not just for ourselves, but everyone that will read this.

We want to thank the many great storytellers that came before us, specifically Eiichiro Oda, Hiromu Arakawa, Michael Dante DiMartino, and Bryan Konietzko. We would not be the storytellers that we are without the inspiration of One Piece, Fullmetal Alchemist, and Avatar the Last Airbender. You set the stage, now we hope to stand up there with you.

I also want to thank my wife for all the support she's shown me through these years. Through the late night writing sessions, encouraging me every step of the way, offering me insights to the process, and celebrating every win we've had in creating this. She has truly been there for me when I've doubted myself the most.

– Mark

About the Authors

Shae Moloney lives in Minnesota and falsely believes the sub-zero-degree winters have made her a more resilient person. Shae's been telling stories her whole life, and when she's not writing professionally or recreationally, it's because she's being interrupted by her dog Lup. Her other published or recognized short fiction work includes *Practice Makes Perfect*, *The Neighborhood*, *On the Other Side,* and *Cowboys After Dinner.*

Kyle Keller has been staring at the inky black night sky and dreaming of fantastical worlds since he was old enough to have his first existential crisis. Since then, he hasn't stopped feverishly scrawling his stories onto any medium he could get his hands on from film, tv, books, comics, music, and digital. Kyle loves creating entertainment and bringing the characters in his mind to life in our world. Somehow he convinced Mark and Shae, two of the most talented people in the world, to be his lifelong creative partners and he is all the better for it. This book and all of his ideas would not exist without them.

Mark Sidener has worked in the film industry over the last 14 years, exploring many different creative projects in that medium. During that time, he co-founded Outer Giant Studios with his best friend Kyle Keller to take their creative spirits to the next level! Some would say over level 9000. As an avid lover of all things anime, Mark currently binges countless series with his beloved cat Ms. Peaches when he's not working on his own stories.

Thank you so much for reading

HYPER OBJECT

Volume 1

We'd like to extend a special thanks to:

Matt Owen
Nickie Henk
Sara Carolynn Kennedy
Kyla Finn
Lydia Sansom
Vik Govindarajan
Alex Bosch
Randi Nimz
Jay Ryan
Chris Little
Richard Nguyen
Octavianus Gozali
Kate Leonardo

For helping make this story a reality.

Thank you,
Kyle, Mark, & Shae

Back to work, ya Mite!

outer
giant

Follow Us

@outergiant

Read more Hyper Object at:

hyperobject.ink

Join our mailing list to receive alerts
on our latest releases and deals.

outergiant.com

Go give this book to your friend!